Candy Apple books...
just for you.
Sweet. Fresh. Fun.
Take a bite!

by Lisa Papademetriou

SCHOLASTIC INC.

New York Toronto London Auckland Sydney
Mexico City New Delhi Hong Kong Buenos Aires

ISBN-13: 978-0-545-13212-1
ISBN-10: 0-545-13212-6

Copyright © 2008 by Lisa Papademetriou

12 11 10 9 8 7 6 5 4 3 2 1   9 10 11 12 13 14/0
Printed in the U.S.A.
First printing, January 2009

For Miliann,
who always knows what to say,
and for Sangha,
who always appreciates
the funny parts

CHAPTER ONE

What's Hot, What's Not: A List by Amy Flowers
In: Celery green
Out: Jealousy green

"Okay, Amy, step back. You've handed out twice as many booklets as me," said my good friend Michiko Ohara as she leaned toward the heavyset woman who had just walked through the wide double doors. "Program?" Mitchie smiled, holding out a green booklet.

The woman lifted her eyebrows and gave the booklet in Mitchie's hand a pinched look. "Thank you, dear," she said primly. Then she floated away in a swirl of vibrant blue chiffon and glittery beads.

We were standing at the entrance to a fancy ballroom, greeting people as they arrived at the

1

fund-raiser my mom had organized for the Save the Earth Foundation, where she works. Our friend Kiwi Adair was there, too. So was my older brother, Kirk. Our job was to hand out guide-books to the items that people would bid on later in the live auction. Mom had really done a great job — she'd persuaded some of the coolest places in Houston to donate stuff, including a private party from La Luxe spa and a seven-night cruise up the Nile in Egypt from Livingston Travel.

"I love the color of that dress," I said as a woman in red floated past. The fabric flowed like liquid around the woman's ankles.

"How much do you think it cost?" Mitchie asked no one in particular.

"Thirteen hundred dollars retail," Kiwi answered.

I raised an eyebrow at her.

"We just got one in the store," Kiwi explained. "It still had the tags on." Kiwi's parents own the most exclusive thrift — I mean, consignment — shop in Houston. It's an awesome place to shop. In fact, it's where I scored the soft green velvet jacket I was wearing at that moment.

My older brother, Kirk, watched the woman in the blue dress make her way across the room toward one of the silent auction tables, where people could write down how much they'd pay for each item. "I really like her helmet," he said, eyeing her perfectly coiffed white hairdo. I had to admit that the hair did look kind of . . . bulletproof.

Mitchie cracked up. "Military chic is really in this year," she shot back.

Kirk grinned at her. "Is that why so many people came in uniform?" he asked, nodding at two women who were wearing the exact same pink dress. They were both standing at a silent auction table, about to bid on a pet party from Pampered Pooch.

A few more people arrived, and we handed out programs. This was the Save the Earth Foundation's gala event, and everyone was dressed super elegantly. The Waldorf Hotel had donated the space for the auction, and Mom had decorated the tables with beautiful green tablecloths, white candles in green holders, and large green-and-white flower arrangements. The theme of the auction was "Let's Get Green," because Mom's foundation is trying to save the planet. That's why I had on a green jacket, green tights, and a vintage green sequined skirt. Naturally, Kirk had said, "Are you off to the Emerald City?" the minute he saw my outfit. But I wasn't the only one in green — Mitchie had on a green satin shirt and black pants, and Kiwi was wearing a yellow dress with green trim.

"How's everything going?" Mom asked as she hurried over to us. Her dress was a delicate mint-green. A few tendrils had escaped from the bun at the back of her neck, and she nervously shoved her glasses farther up onto her nose. "Do you have enough programs? Does anyone need something to eat? You can take turns heading over to the buffet, if you want. The live auction should start in a few minutes."

"We're good, Mom," I told her, touching her arm gently. "Relax."

She flashed me a grateful smile and darted off to check on the silent auction.

"I'm hitting the buffet," Kirk said, plopping his programs onto a nearby table. "Who wants one of those flaky cheese things?" Kirk had hit the buffet a couple of times already.

"I do," Mitchie told him. "And would you get me a few cherry tomatoes, with some of that dip? And maybe a couple of crackers with that good cheese? Oh, and I'm dying of thirst — could you get me a drink? That orange seltzer water is good."

4

"Do I look like I brought a wheelbarrow?" Kirk teased. "Why don't you just come with me?"

"Go ahead," I said when Mitchie glanced at me. I knew that she had to leave the party early. "Kiwi and I can handle things here for a while."

Mitchie smiled. "Cool! Be back in a few." Then she and Kirk bopped off toward the food table.

Just then, I heard Kiwi make an annoyed little clicking sound with her teeth, and when I turned around, I saw why. Fiona Von Steig had just walked in. She went to our school, Allington Academy, and thought of herself as the Queen Bee. Though Queen *Bug* would be more accurate.

She and her best friends were known as the League. As in, "They're out of your league." Nice, right?

Fiona was with a very slender frosted-blond woman and an older man with silver hair who was texting something on a BlackBerry. Her parents, I guessed. Both of them looked as if they spent all day at the country club, tanning and playing endless rounds of golf and tennis.

"Hi, Fiona," I said as I held out a program. Fiona just lifted an eyebrow, then accepted the booklet between her thumb and forefinger, as if it was coated in germs. I think she was still mad at me for the prank I'd pulled on her a few weeks before.

5

She was supposed to pop out of a glass box as a magic trick at her birthday party, but I'd kind of . . . well . . . glued the box shut. Not that she had liked me much before that, but still . . .

Fiona scanned the room. "I thought St. Patrick's Day was in March," she said snidely.

"It's a green theme," I explained. "Because Save the Earth is an environmental cause." I gave Fiona's parents a big smile. After all, this was my mother's event.

"How adorable," her mother said. Somehow, though, Mrs. Von Steig made "adorable" sound like "vomit-inducing." *Well, at least now I know where Fiona gets her charm.*

Fiona's father looked up from his BlackBerry. "Can we please get this over with?" he asked his wife. "Honestly, I don't know why you make me come to these things. Why can't I just write a check and stay at the office?"

"Because we have to mingle," Mrs. Von Steig replied. "It's *important* for people to think we care about the environment." With that, Fiona's family strode into the room, with Mr. Von Steig grumbling the whole way.

Just then, a loud voice boomed. "There she is!" A moment later, my uncle Steve appeared. "Hey!" Spotting my green outfit, he grinned hugely.

"Where's your pot of gold buried?" he asked in his best leprechaun voice.

"You can bid on it at table three," I told him, giggling a little. Funny how the same joke from Fiona made me want to strangle her . . . but from Uncle Steve, it made me laugh.

"Hey, Amy!" Jenelle said, giving me a huge smile. She turned to a woman in a short, sophisticated black dress. "Mom, you remember Amy, right?"

"Who could forget Amy?" Uncle Steve added. He isn't my real uncle, by the way. He's my dad's best friend.

"Nice to see you again," I said. Linda is engaged to Uncle Steve, and Jenelle is a friend of mine. Unfortunately, she's also best friends with Fiona, which makes things complicated.

"Of course I remember you," Jenelle's mom said with a laugh. She had a wide smile and the same large hazel eyes as Jenelle. "Isn't this gorgeous?" she gushed, looking around the room. "Green! For the environment — how *clever*. I hear your mother is in charge of this event, Amy."

"She sure is." I blushed a little, even though I was proud.

"Well, she's done a great job," Linda said. "And

I just love your outfit! You look as fresh as a spring leaf! Doesn't she, Steve?"

"Like a tree!" he agreed, wrapping an arm around his fiancée. "A leafy tree!" He smiled, his eyes dancing.

"Oh, Jenelle, you're finally here," Fiona said as she walked over to join us. "I've been waiting for you *forever*."

I rolled my eyes, debating whether or not to tell Jenelle that Fiona had arrived exactly forty-five seconds before she had.

"Sorry," Jenelle told her. "Mom couldn't find her car keys."

"In my handbag!" Linda said brightly. "The last place I looked." She turned back to me. "So, Amy, you go to Allington Academy, too, right?"

"I just started this year," I told her.

"Hm . . . Hm . . ." She put a finger to her lips and looked up at Uncle Steve. "Do you know what I'm thinking?"

"I think I do!" Steve said, grinning. It was cute to see him standing with Linda. They both had round faces and bright eyes, and they reminded me of cartoon daffodils — the kind that smile and sing.

"Amy, I'm having a fashion show at my store next weekend," Linda said.

I nodded. Linda owns Bounce, the coolest teen boutique in Houston. I'd only been there once before, but I knew I loved the clothes.

"One of our models just had to cancel," she went on. "Would you like to take her place?"

"What?" I squeaked. "Me?"

"Her?" Fiona muttered under her breath. "What's Bounce selling — the Nerd Look?"

Linda didn't catch what Fiona said, but I did. And Jenelle shot her a glare.

I felt myself blushing harder. Which was bad news. My cheeks turn bright red with a white dot in the center, which gives me a very unappealing clown look and makes me even more self-conscious. "It's just that I've never modeled before —"

"I can help you," Jenelle volunteered. "It's easy. It's just walking."

"Jenelle's an old pro," Linda said. "She and Fiona have done this two years in a row!"

Fiona narrowed her eyes at me dangerously and gave her head a tiny shake. I felt like I could practically read her mind: *Queen Bug says no.* The funny thing is that I'd been about to refuse . . . but the minute Fiona gave me that look, I knew I had to say yes. "Sounds great!" I said brightly.

"Fantastic!" Linda leaned over and gave me a kiss on the cheek. "You'll be wonderful, I know it."

Fiona rolled her eyes as Linda and Steve headed off. "Just don't screw this up, Amy," Fiona warned me. "Or you'll seriously regret it. Come on, Jenelle." Then she stalked away toward the punch bowl.

Jenelle hesitated a minute. "Don't worry," she whispered in my ear. "It'll be fun, I promise." Then she gave me a smile and hurried off after Fiona.

I turned to Kiwi, who hadn't said a word the entire time. "Well, that should be interesting," she said with a laugh.

I rolled my eyes. "Maybe I should have said no —"

"And missed the chance to irk Fiona?" Kiwi looked shocked. "Never!"

"What did we miss?" Mitchie asked as she and Kirk joined us. She was holding a plate piled high with food and had a glass of orange soda in one hand.

"Fiona's head just nearly exploded because Amy's going to be in the Bounce fashion show," Kiwi announced.

Mitchie — who had just taken a sip of her soda — had to spit it back into the glass. "What?"

she screeched, looking delighted. She and Fiona have a History.

"Who's Fiona?" Kirk asked.

"Forget it," I told him.

At that moment, a gorgeous Asian girl poked her head in through the double doors. "Mitchie?" she said. "Mom asked me to pick you up. Are you ready?"

"You're here already?" Mitchie looked disappointed.

"Sorry, but you know Mom." Mitchie's sister stepped through the doors, but only barely. She wasn't dressed up — she was just wearing a denim skirt and a Yale sweatshirt — but she was one of the prettiest people I'd ever seen. She looked better than ninety-nine percent of the dressed-up people in the room.

"Hi, I'm Kirk!" My brother's eyes were lit up like Christmas-tree bulbs.

Mitchie rolled her eyes.

"I'm Akina." She turned back to Mitchie. "You've got orange soda on your shirt, by the way."

Mitchie looked down at her shirt in horror. "Mom's going to kill me!"

"So true. You ready?"

"Sorry, Amy," Mitchie said, her mouth twisting wistfully as she placed her food and drink on a nearby table. "It's my grandmother's birthday tomorrow, and we've got to get up super-early to drive to San Antonio. I've got to —"

"No problem," I told her. "Thanks for helping out." I gave her a hug. She hugged Kiwi, too, then Akina held open the door for her. Mitchie waved good-bye.

"Nice meeting you, Akina!" Kirk called.

Akina didn't turn around. She just gave him a backwards wave over her shoulder.

"Wow," Kirk said, leaning against the table. "Wow."

"You realize that you just put your hand in Mitchie's veggie dip," I told him.

"Oh, shoot!" Kirk grabbed a napkin. "Shoot, shoot, shoot!" he said as he wiped the green goop from his drippy hand.

"It's okay," Kiwi told him. "Akina always has that effect on people."

Kirk ignored her, but I wondered what it was about people like Akina and Fiona. I mean, there are other good-looking people in the world. But not all of them can make people's brains turn to pudding.

That's one superpower I'd like to have.

*   *   *

"Are you sure that's right?" My lab partner, Anderson Sempe, frowned at the notes I'd just written down. It was Wednesday, which was usually an easy day in science class — quizzes and tests were always on Mondays. But Mr. Pearl had already turned off his PowerPoint presentation, and, as usual, Anderson hadn't had time to copy down the last page. "How can sound travel faster in water than in air? You can hardly hear anything when you're underwater."

"Sound is a wave," I explained. "It travels faster through liquids or solids." At that moment, the bell chimed, letting us know it was time for our next class.

Anderson's blue eyes rolled toward the ceiling. "Did you hear that?" he demanded. "Are you telling me I'd be able to hear that better if, like, my head was surrounded by a giant rock?" He pressed his palm flat against the smooth black marble top of our lab table, as if trying to imagine his skull encased in granite. The labs at Allington Academy were gorgeous, fitted with stainless steel sinks and gleaming equipment. At my old school, we had beat-up wooden tables and microscopes from the Paleolithic Era. I'd been at Allington for weeks, but I still couldn't help comparing the two schools.

It was kind of funny, really. For me, coming to class was a luxury experience. But everyone else at Allington just took all of that stuff — the elegant old buildings, the free laptop for every student, the lush green grounds, the school bus with a TV screen on the back of every plush seat — for granted. Like right now, Anderson was staring at the black granite, but he wasn't really seeing it. He was just seeing a slab of stone. "You can't hear through rock!" Anderson insisted.

"Give it up, Andy." Preston Harringford leaned lazily against our lab table. His backpack was slung carelessly over one shoulder, and he hiked it a little higher as he added, "There's no point in arguing with Amy. Just be glad that she's sitting next to you." He smirked at me. Preston had been teasing me for a week because Mr. Pearl made a huge deal when I got the highest grade in the class on the first exam. Let me tell you one thing — I never would have answered that extra credit question if I'd known it was going to create so much misery. Preston continued, "She's a *genius*, right, Amy?"

"I'm smart enough to be able to copy down what Mr. Pearl says," I shot back. Then I immediately felt like a jerk because, of course, it takes Anderson a long time to copy down the notes, and

I hadn't meant to insult him. That was the thing about Preston — he really irked me. And when people irk me, I say dumb things, which only irks me more. It's a horrible cycle of irksome dumbness, and the only way to fight it is to shut up entirely. Which is what I did.

"Oh, come on," Preston teased. "Anyone can tell you're brilliant. Just look at the pencil sticking out of your skull."

I felt the back of my head. Sure enough, I'd twisted my hair into a bun and fastened it with a pencil. I do that sometimes when I'm thinking hard. I don't even notice it, until I can't find my pencil.

"Ms. Flowers!" Mr. Pearl called from the front of the classroom. "May I speak with you for a minute? Quick, quick, quick!" He opened his huge eyes wide and snapped his fingers in my direction. Coming from anyone else, it would have seemed kind of rude, but with Mr. Pearl, I knew it was just the five cups of coffee talking.

"Just a sec," I said, slipping my book into my bag.

"Must be time to get your Genius Award."

I narrowed my eyes at Preston's back as he laughed and walked off. "Jeez, he's annoying," I said as he slipped out the door.

"Really?" Anderson asked as if the thought had never occurred to him. His blue eyes were wide and bright, like clear pools of water. "I think Preston's funny." That's the thing about Anderson — he really just sees the good in people.

Rolling my eyes, I hurried to the front of the class.

"Amy Flowers," Mr. Pearl singsonged, interlacing his fingers over his large belly and leaning back in his chair. "Amy Flowers, how would you like to take part in an exciting extracurricular activity? Hm?" Before I had a chance to answer he added, "What if I told you that it came with extra credit and a chance to be on TV?"

"Does it involve dancing with the stars?" I asked him.

"Dancing?" Mr. Pearl's bug-like eyes popped so wide I thought they might jump out of his head. "Ha-ha! No, no — of course not! It involves the far more glamorous world of *science*! Yes, yes! The Academic Challenge is coming up, and it seems to me that someone with the highest test score in the class — in the entire grade, mind you — deserves a slot on the team. We need a science person — and Amy Flowers, that's you!"

I cocked my head. "What's the Academic Challenge?"

"What's the —" Mr. Pearl smacked a large hand across his forehead and drew his fingers down his face in dismay. "Oh, my goodness, how can you not know the Challenge? It's a contest of wits! A brain slugfest! A battle to find the best school in the city of Houston! Teams of four students answer tough questions on a variety of subjects — math, science, literature, history, geography, foreign language. Allington used to win it year after year. But for the past few years," he narrowed his eyes and dropped his voice, "we've lost to *Karter*." There was real horror on his face. Karter is Allington's biggest rival . . . in everything. Soccer, football, and — apparently — academics. "And the worst part is that the final round is on television," Mr. Pearl went on, shaking his head sadly. "Imagine it! All of those people watching as we lost to Karter! Well, I've sworn that won't happen this year. We must bring the glory back to Allington!" He pounded a fist against his wooden desk.

"Sounds like fun," I told him.

"Fun?" Mr. Pearl thought that over.

"Isn't it?" I asked.

Mr. Pearl shrugged. "Okay, why not? It'll be lots of fun! So, you're on the team?"

"Sure."

"Wonderful, Amy! Ten extra credit points on your next quiz!" His fingers flew across the keyboard as he typed a note to himself. "First official meeting is next Monday."

"I'll be there," I told him. My hair tumbled across my shoulders as I pulled the pencil from my bun and made a note in my calendar. When I turned to leave, I saw that Anderson was chatting with Jenelle. They were leaning toward each other slightly, and Jenelle's eyes were bright. I couldn't help smiling a little. I knew they had *serious* crushes on each other.

"Um, hel-lo?" Fiona said, tapping her foot impatiently. "Jenelle, are you coming to art class, or what?" She gave her long black hair an impatient shake.

"Oh, uh, yeah," Jenelle said quickly. "See you, Anderson."

"See you," he said as Jenelle trotted after Fiona.

With a slow smile, Anderson walked over to join me.

"She's such a pain," I told him, glaring at Fiona's disappearing back.

"Fiona?" Anderson shrugged. "Eh, she's okay. She can be really funny sometimes. And she's super-smart."

I sighed as he and I stepped into the hall. "Anderson, why are you so nice all the time?" I demanded. "Don't you ever just — get mad? Isn't there anybody you just don't like?"

Anderson pressed his lips together. "Not really," he admitted.

I couldn't help laughing a little. "I sure wish I felt that way," I told him.

"You guys, guess what?" Mitchie said, dumping her tray on the table with a clatter. She slid into the seat next to Kiwi. "Ms. Lusk just asked me to be on the Academic Challenge team!"

Kiwi let out a muffled squeal — her mouth was full of sweet potato fries.

I swear, the Allington cafeteria has some of the best food in Houston. I was eating a bowl of perfectly spiced seafood gumbo and a side salad of mesclun greens. There was a small dish of crème brûlée on my tray for dessert, the custard sweet and creamy beneath its glass ceiling of glazed sugar. And the food was included in tuition, which — since I was on a full scholarship — meant it was completely free for me.

Kiwi finished chewing her fries, swallowed, and grinned. "Amy's on it, too!"

Mitchie's huge smile got even huger. "You *are*? That rocks!" She held up her palm, and I high-fived it.

"Mr. Pearl asked me," I said. I'd just finished telling Kiwi all about it.

"Fabulous! We needed a good science person!" Mitchie nibbled the end of a bright green asparagus spear. "We've just *got* to win it this year." Her dark eyes were bright. "We *can't* lose to Karter again — I'll never hear the end of it."

I looked at Kiwi, who nodded sympathetically.

"Wait — what's the big deal?" I asked. "I mean, it would be better to win, of course. But if we come in second in the city, it doesn't seem like the world will come to an end."

Mitchie looked at me sharply. "It will for *me*," she said.

"Akina was on the team the last year that they won the championship," Kiwi explained as she drew her fingers through the ends of her waist-length auburn hair. "It must be hard to have a perfect older sister," Kiwi said gently.

"She's not perfect," Mitchie snapped. "It's just that everybody thinks she is." Kiwi winced a little, and Mitchie's face softened. "Sorry," she said quickly. "It's just — *frustrating*."

I nodded, trying to imagine what it would be like to have an older sibling who was good at everything. Honestly, Kirk's grades just make me look good.

Mitchie shook her head like a dog shaking off a bath. Mitchie has really glossy chin-length black hair, and when she shakes it, it always falls right back into place. If I did that to my hair, I'd look like a giant lint ball. "Anyway, it doesn't matter, because we're going to win — right, Amy?"

"I hope so," I told her.

"What?" Mitchie opened her mouth, mock-scandalized. She pointed her fork in my direction. "We're going to win! Say it! Say it or I'll — I'll take your honey-wheat roll!"

I cupped my hands protectively around the roll at the edge of my salad plate. "Not the roll!" I cried. "Okay, okay — we're definitely going to win."

"That's better." Mitchie smiled at me, satisfied, and plucked a fry from Kiwi's plate.

"Wait — now you're stealing *my* food instead?" Kiwi demanded. "What did I do?"

Mitchie gave her a playful grin. "Eh, you're just

an innocent bystander. Those fries are awesome, by the way."

"You want more?" Kiwi asked. "I'm done with them."

"Sure." Mitchie reached toward the plate and shoved two fries into her mouth. "Mmm."

"Hey, guys," said a voice behind me.

"Hey, Jenelle." She was hovering at the edge of the table uncertainly, like she wasn't sure she'd be welcome or not. I gestured to the empty seat beside me. "Want to join us?"

"Oh, I just dropped by for a second," Jenelle said, tucking a lock of bouncy blond hair behind one ear.

"What happened?" Mitchie asked dryly. "You got lost? The Dahlia Room is on the other side of the DC." The dining center is divided up into separate, smaller rooms, each named for a flower. Right now, we were sitting in the Sunflower Room, which was painted a cheerful yellow with white trim. But the League never sat anywhere but the maroon-and-black Dahlia Room.

Jenelle didn't actually reply — she just gave Mitchie a tight little smile. I felt my own smile freeze up on my face. I really liked Mitchie, and I really liked Jenelle. But they didn't like each other. At all.

22

Kiwi lifted her glass of seltzer water to her lips, but her eyes were traveling from Mitchie to Jenelle and back again. She hates arguments even more than I do.

"Listen, Amy, I just wanted to know if you had some time to hang out on Saturday," Jenelle said. "I thought we could go over a few modeling tricks before the Bounce show."

"Sure," I said. "I could —"

"Actually, Amy has to study on Saturday," Mitchie put in, cutting me off. "The Academic Challenge team is getting together."

What? This was the first I was hearing about a team meeting.

"I think Amy can speak for herself," Jenelle shot back.

"Fine." Mitchie waved a hand in my direction. "She'll tell you."

"I didn't actually know that we had a team meeting," I confessed. "I thought the first meeting was Monday."

"There's an unofficial meeting on Saturday from two to five," Mitchie informed me. "We're meeting at Daily Blend." She folded her arms across her chest and gave Jenelle a defiant glare.

"Oh," I said. "Well, um, maybe we could meet before then?" I suggested, looking up at Jenelle.

She was looking at Mitchie with a slightly pink face, as if anger was rising to a slow boil inside her cheeks. "Like at noon?"

It took a moment for what I'd said to penetrate Jenelle's anger force-field. "What?" she said, looking at me suddenly. "I'm sorry. Did you say something?"

"I said that maybe you could come over to my house at noon," I repeated. "I'll work on modeling for a couple of hours, then meet Mitchie at Daily Blend."

"Fine," Jenelle said.

Mitchie shrugged. "Fine."

Kiwi blew out a sigh and placed her empty glass back onto her tray. "Great!" She sounded as relieved as I felt.

"See you later, Amy," Jenelle said, turning on her heel. She didn't say anything to Mitchie or Kiwi.

"Toodles," Michie called sarcastically after Jenelle's retreating figure, but Jenelle didn't stop or turn back. Or even break her stride. Mitchie blew out a breath that sent her dark bangs fluttering over her eyebrows. "I swear, Amy, I don't know why you're friends with that girl."

"She's nice," I said simply.

"She's in the League." Mitchie's e[yes locked] onto mine. "You don't know her as w[ell as you] think you do."

I thought about that for a moment. Jene[lle had] always been friendly toward me. Then agai[n, her] best friend was someone I couldn't stand....

"Maybe I don't," I admitted.

Still, I wasn't about to give up on Jenelle. Not yet, anyway.

CHAPTER TWO

In: Pointy black pencils
Out: Pointy black shoes

"Okay, before I watch you walk," Jenelle said as she perched at the edge of our green couch, "you should probably put these on." It was Saturday morning, and Jenelle had arrived five minutes early. I was a little surprised that she wanted to get to work on the modeling stuff right away. "There's so much to go over!" she said.

"Really?" I asked. "I thought you said it was just walking."

"Believe me, it's harder than it looks," Jenelle replied. She reached into the shopping bag she had brought with her and pulled out a shoe box.

26

Inside was a pair of black shoes with the narrowest, highest heels I'd ever seen.

"Am I supposed to walk in these?" I joked, holding out a shoe heel first. "Or just use them to defend myself from potential attackers?"

A smile crept up the side of Jenelle's face. "You're supposed to walk in them, unfortunately."

With a small sigh, I plopped down onto the sofa next to her. I kicked off my purple Mary Jane clogs and slipped my feet into the shoes, wincing. My toes felt as if they were caught in a vise. "Foot torture," I said — and then I stood up. "Whoa!" I cried, windmilling my arms. I had to grab on to the arm of the couch to keep from flopping over in a heap. "This is going to be a little more challenging than I thought," I said, straightening up. A horrible image of myself tumbling off the catwalk floated through my mind.

Jenelle nodded. "Tell me about it. But at least they aren't high-heeled mules. I accidentally kicked one into the audience once." She stood up and took my hands to help me balance. "Okay, the secret is to walk mostly on your toes. Don't put too much weight on the heel."

"Okay." I took a few ginger steps across the

family-room floor. "Okay, not so bad," I said. I walked around the two recliners, circling the room. I came to a stop in front of Jenelle, who was frowning. "What?"

Jenelle tapped a finger against her lower lip, thoughtfully. She was wearing a really pretty shade of pale peach polish, and I suddenly felt self-conscious about my ragged cuticles and uneven nails. I made a mental note: *Paint nails before fashion show*. I was sure the rest of the models would have nice hands — especially the League. "You have a very bouncy walk," Jenelle said finally.

"I do?" I asked.

"You sort of bob your head and pull up on your heels," Jenelle explained. "Like you're listening to a song in your head."

"I *am* listening to a song in my head," I admitted. I can't help it — everything makes me think of music. Like, right then, just walking around the room made me think of the song "Walking on Sunshine," this 1980s hit that's one of my dad's favorites.

"Well, try to make it a slow song," Jenelle suggested. "You want people to have enough time to look at the clothes. More like this." She straightened her spine and walked around the room. As she walked, I found myself noticing her clothes. Jenelle had on a short black-and-red patterned skirt and a white T-shirt. It wasn't a fancy outfit, but the way she moved made it look different — better. I tried to pay attention to what she was doing. Her head didn't bounce at all. "That's called the 'catwalk strut,'" Jenelle explained. "You try it."

"Like this?" I asked. I froze my head at the top of my neck and tried to slip my legs out in front of me delicately, as if they were antennae. I tried to remember to walk on my tiptoes and I thought of the slowest relevant song I could: "Amazing Grace." I steered around the coffee table and made my way back to Jenelle. "How was that?"

She pressed her lips together. "Um . . ."

"Because I felt like a robot," I admitted.

Jenelle laughed. "Yeah," she said with a slight blush. "Though I was thinking more zombie. Okay, maybe we'll come back to the walk. Let's try something easier." She flipped her hair behind her shoulders and said, "When you walk down the catwalk, you don't want to smile. You want to look a little . . . blank. Again, it's about getting people to look at the clothes, not you."

"Okay . . ."

"This is called the 'fashion frown,'" Jenelle explained. She tilted her head slightly, pursed her lips just a little, and looked at the wall with her lids half closed. She did that for a full thirty seconds, then turned to me. "Try it."

I tried to make my face as blank as possible, drooped my eyelids, and pursed my lips. "Like this?" I asked through my pursed lips. It came out sounding a bit like, "Mike wis?"

Jenelle bit her lip, but a voice from the doorway said, "You look like you're trying to hold your breath for the world record." Kirk sauntered over to the couch and flopped his feet onto the coffee table.

I looked at Jenelle. "Really?"

She winced a bit. "Well, maybe more like you were . . . concentrating. Like you were trying to mentally multiply four hundred thirty-seven by sixty-two." Kirk gave a little laugh-snort as Jenelle went on. "Try to relax your facial muscles a little."

"What are you guys doing?" Kirk asked, leaning back against the side of the couch to watch us. "Trying to move things with the power of your brains?"

"We're practicing for the Bounce fashion show," I explained. "Jenelle is showing me how to walk."

Kirk snorted. "Good luck. I once saw Amy fall off a curb — while standing still."

"Kirk, do you mind?" I asked. "We need to use this room."

"The game's on in five minutes," he protested, clicking the remote. The TV screen burst to life with a roaring crowd. "Play-offs!"

"Well, where am I supposed to practice walking?" I demanded.

"Hit the street," Kirk suggested.

I glared at him.

"What about the living room?" he demanded.

"Mom's book club is up there," I pointed out.

"We can head up to your room," Jenelle suggested. "We can practice turning next. We don't need a lot of space." She took a step forward and pivoted slowly, to demonstrate. "You do that at the end of the catwalk," she explained. "Step right, shift your weight, pivot, step left."

I put out my right foot and tried to imitate her. "Step right," I said, "shift my weight — whoops!"

Jenelle reached out and caught me before I hit the floor like a sack of rocks. I glared down at my feet. *I hate you, shoes*, I thought. *And, feet, you aren't helping, either!*

"Wow, you really *do* need to practice walking," Kirk said, sitting up. "I thought you were kidding when you said that."

"Well, I wasn't," I snapped.

"She *really* wasn't," Jenelle agreed. I looked at her, and she caught herself. "I mean, you're doing great, really. You just need to practice."

"Okay, okay," Kirk said, clicking off the TV. "I'll go watch the game at Todd's." Todd is one of Kirk's best friends — he lives across the street, and they hang out together all of the time.

"Thanks, Kirk," Jenelle said. "That's really sweet of you."

"Eh, no big." Kirk flapped his hand, as if to say, *Whatever — I'm always a totally generous guy.* "Just call me Mr. Wonderful!" he joked.

"Oh, but I can think of so many *other* nicknames for you," I teased.

Kirk laughed and headed for the stairs. "Good luck learning to walk," he called over his shoulder. "Try not to break your neck."

"I'll do my best," I muttered, sneaking a glance at Jenelle's eager face. *Well, at least someone is still feeling good about this lesson*, I thought.

That makes one of us.

* * *

"Sorrysorrysorrysorrysorrysorrysorry!" I said as I slipped into the grass-green booth beside Mitchie. After Jenelle taught me how to turn, she had me walk around with a pile of books on my head. Then she had me watch a few videos of professional models on the catwalk. That part was fun, actually . . . but I completely lost track of time, and now I was late for my first Academic Challenge meeting. Luckily, I only live about three blocks from Daily Blend — I ran the whole way. "Sorry I'm late —" The table was piled high with books and index cards — the rest of the team had already started without me.

"It's okay," Mitchie said. "We were really just getting started. Amy, do you know everybody?"

"Hi, Amy," said a shy voice from the corner of the booth. Scott Lawson was smiling at me with dreamy chocolate-brown eyes.

"Oh, hi!" I tried to sound chipper as my heart gave a flutter. A trickle of sweat inched down my neck, and I regretted running to the meeting. I probably looked horrible — and I didn't even want to think about how I *smelled*. If I'd known Scott was on the team, I definitely would have been on time.

Scott and I had danced together at Fiona's birthday party — the same party where I locked her in the glass box — but we hadn't seen much of each other since then. He's in the grade above me at Allington, so we don't have any classes together.

"And this is Arielle," Mitchie said, gesturing to a pretty girl with dark cocoa skin and long hair.

"Nice to meet you," I said. "Sorry I'm late."

"It's not a big deal even though I got here fifteen minutes early; I always do that, I always get places early and then everyone else is late, so I just sit and read a book, which is why I always have a novel or some other interesting book with me in my bag, like for example right now, I'm reading *Tess of the d'Urbervilles*, because according to the American Testing Service, it's one of the novels that appears on national tests most often." Arielle took a sip of the pink smoothie in front of her. Wow, I'd never met anyone who could talk so quickly. *If this contest has a speed round, we're golden*, I thought.

"Arielle's our alternate," Mitchie explained.

"I thought that there were four people on the team," I said, just as Preston Harringford walked up carrying three smoothies.

34

"Well, look who finally made it!" he said as he passed a purple smoothie to Scott and an orange one to Mitchie. "Our resident genius has finally arrived! I guess we can start now."

"You know Preston, right?" Mitchie asked, turning in her seat to face me. "He's our fourth."

"He *is*?"

"Don't look so shocked." Preston smirked. "You aren't the only one with a brain around here, you know."

"I'm sorry — I didn't mean —" I shook my head. *What* did *I mean?* It was just — I'd never realized that Preston was smart enough for something like the Academic Challenge.

"Preston is our geography guy," Mitchie explained. "And he speaks six foreign languages."

"You *do*?"

"Ik ben een en al verrassing," Preston replied.

"Is that Swedish?" Scott asked.

"Dutch," Preston replied. "It means, 'I'm just full of surprises.'" He leaned back against the plush faux-leather booth and grinned at me. "Actually, I really only speak four foreign languages fluently — Dutch, Italian, French, and German. But I know a little Spanish, too, and I can speak some Arabic. But I can't write it at all, or read it, either, so don't ask me."

Okay, I knew that my jaw was hanging open. But I couldn't help it! I felt as if I'd just discovered that Bozo the Clown and Albert Einstein were the same person. "How did you learn so many languages?" I asked him.

Preston shrugged. *"I miei genitori sono diplomatici."*

"Oh, I take Italian, I know what that means," Arielle gushed. "It means your parents are diplomats — wow, that must be so cool! My dad's just a regular old businessman and who cares about that?"

"I guess it's cool," Preston said. "If you don't mind moving all the time."

"Okay, back to work," Mitchie said, reaching for a pile of index cards. "Anyone on the team can answer any of the questions, but we're all here because we've got certain strengths. We know why Preston's here, I'm good at literature and history, Amy's got a science brain, and Scott is good at math."

"And I'm good at everything," Arielle said quickly. "So if any of you get sick, it's no big deal."

I had to work hard to not roll my eyes. Arielle

looked really eager — as if she was secretly hoping that one of us would come down with bubonic plague or something.

"Okay." Mitchie mashed her lips together as she peered at the first index card. "Mr. Pearl said the easiest ones are on top. . . . First question: What is a tesseract?"

My heart thrummed in my ears and I felt my face burn. *Is that a science question?* I hoped not. I had no idea what a tesseract was. *Maybe it's a foreign language question.* I hoped, hoped, hoped it wasn't for me. I didn't want to look like an idiot in front of Scott. Or — even worse — Preston.

"It's a four-dimensional analog of a cube," Scott answered.

I felt the air whoosh out of me. Honestly, I had no idea what that meant — but Scott did, and that was all that mattered.

"Great." Mitchie made a note on the card and moved on to the next. "Okay. Identify this quote: 'What a piece of work is man, how noble in reason.'" Mitchie rolled her eyes. "Ea-sy," she singsonged. "It's from Shakespeare's *Hamlet.* Wow, I hope these get a little harder. I'd love to see what Karter is studying."

I wanted to say that *I* thought the question was pretty hard. But I just glanced at Scott and kept quiet. He smiled at me, and I felt like my head had just been dipped in warm bathwater.

Mitchie flipped to another card. "Here's one for you, Amy. Question: The word "electricity" comes from the Greek word *elektron*. What does *elektron* mean?"

All of that nice warmth in my head leaked away immediately, and I felt like I was circling the drain. I had *no* idea how to answer this question. "Um . . ." *Okay, think, think, think!* I commanded myself. *What* could *it mean? It has to be something logical. Electricity, electricity* . . . "Does it mean . . . 'lightning'?"

Mitchie lifted her eyebrows. "No."

"*Elektron* means 'amber,'" Preston piped up from across the table. "But I have no idea why electricity would be named after a clear yellow rock."

"Actually, amber isn't a rock, it's petrified tree sap," Arielle put in, "and William Gilbert used that word because he noticed that if you rubbed a piece of amber with fur, it would attract small particles. You know, static electricity." The corners of her mouth curled into a smug little smile that she aimed in my direction. She took another sip of her smoothie, and I resisted the urge to dump it over her head.

I grimaced. *And that question was from the easy pile! I guess I'd better be on time to the next group meeting*, I thought as Mitchie flipped to the next card. *It looks like I have a lot of studying to do!*

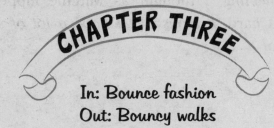

CHAPTER THREE

In: Bounce fashion
Out: Bouncy walks

"Oh, great!" Jenelle said as I poked my head through Bounce's front door the next day. "You're here!" She excused herself from the person she had been chatting with — a tall woman with black hair in a sleek French twist — and wound her way through the chairs that had been set up to the side of the catwalk. "The others are getting ready."

"You look amazing," I said to Jenelle. Her eyes looked enormous, and her hair was even bouncier and fuller than usual.

"Bernard already did my hair and makeup," Jenelle admitted. "He'll do yours, too."

"The store looks so different!" Jenelle led me toward the rear of the store, where a blue curtain had been hung up to create a "backstage" for the fashion show. Racks of clothes had been moved out and chairs had been set up. A guy with a ponytail stood adjusting a camera on a tripod in front of a blue silk ribbon with a sign that read RESERVED FOR PRESS. He was in the front row, where a few seats had special signs on them: TEXAS FABULOUS MAGAZINE, HOUSTON GLAM, ALLINGTON OBSERVER. "The school paper is coming?" I asked. Allington students produced a small glossy magazine on a weekly basis. It was pretty impressive — and everyone read it.

Jenelle shrugged. "It was Fiona's idea. Probably not a bad one, actually. A lot of Allington students shop here."

"I can't believe there used to be a cosmetics display here," I said, pointing to the front corner of the store.

"I know." Jenelle looked over her shoulder to smile at me. "Mom had the place designed so that the displays can be moved around. Everything — even the wooden sweater cases — has wheels. She likes to switch things up." Suddenly, dance music began pulsing through the speakers. It went on for a few beats, then died away. "Sound check,"

Jenelle explained. We walked up to the French-twist-hair woman, who was wearing a short-sleeved orange cashmere sweater and a slim-fitting brown wool skirt. She looked great. "Amy, this is Eva. She manages the store, and she'll be announcing the show."

"Nice to meet you," I said.

"A pleasure." Eva gave me an up-and-down look, and then nodded, as if I passed inspection. Barely.

Jenelle led me backstage, which was surprisingly crowded. Racks of clothes were everywhere, each one labeled with a number, and people with clipboards and headsets were striding from one table to the next. The dressing rooms against the far wall were numbered, too. Three makeup mirrors — the kind surrounded by soft white lights — were set up in the far corner, and a girl was seated at one. Her blue eyes caught mine in the mirror, and I saw that it was Fiona. The third member of the League — Lucia de Leon — was standing beside her, leaning against the makeup table in a maroon wrap dress. A man with a gorgeous silver mane of hair was standing behind Fiona, touching her hair. Linda was with him.

Fiona's eyes flicked away from mine. "I'm just *saying* that this blush is too orange," she told the man with the silver hair. "I look much better in pink. Isn't this blush too orange, Lucia?"

"No offense, but you kind of look like a pumpkin?" Lucia replied in her trademark style. She always raised her voice at the end of every sentence, so it sounded like she was full of questions. "Or like someone dipped you in a vat of Minute Maid?"

Honestly, this was a complete exaggeration. Fiona looked beautiful, and the blush didn't look orange at all. But I knew from experience that there was no point in trying to argue with Fiona once she got an idea into her head. You could either agree . . . or get out of the way.

But there was no way to warn Bernard about this.

"You really have to trust Bernard, Fiona," Linda said patiently. "He's been doing this for years."

"It's not orange," Bernard replied. "It's a gorgeous color for you. Trust me, if we go with something paler, you'll look washed-out under the lights."

43

Fiona folded her arms across her chest. "If you make me wear this color, I'll look *invisible* under the lights because I won't go out there."

"And then, like, the clothes will be hard to see?" Lucia pointed out. "Because, like, they won't be on stage?"

Linda looked horrified, and I could practically read the thoughts running through her mind: *Please don't make me find another model right before the show!*

Bernard's mouth clamped shut, and a blue vein pulsed in his forehead. He glanced at Linda, who raised her hands in a "Work with me" gesture. Finally, Bernard let out a whoosh of breath. "Fine," he snapped. "We'll go with something pink." He spat the word "pink" as if it was half lodged in his throat.

"Great!" Linda said quickly. "Thanks, Bernard, darling, you're always so accommodating." She turned her back to Fiona and heaved a huge sigh. Just then, she caught sight of me and Jenelle, and her face brightened. "Amy, you're here! Wonderful! I hear that Jenelle has been teaching you everything she knows for the show."

"I've been working on it," I told her. "I just hope I don't trip."

I guess Linda didn't realize that I was serious, because she threw her head back and laughed. Then she reached for a clipboard. "Amy, you're model number three. You can find your rack of clothes and dressing room later," she said, using a pen to point to the rooms behind me. "We've got six models. Sasha and Noelle are around here somewhere. And I think you know Fiona and Lucia, right?"

"Hi," I said.

"Hi, Amy," Lucia said, but Fiona just nodded slightly as Bernard finished applying a pale pink blush to her cheeks with a large black makeup brush.

"There you go," he said, placing the brush back into his large tackle box. "Just what you wanted. Pink."

Fiona inspected one cheek, then the other. "It's much better," she announced at last.

Bernard's forehead wrinkled and his lips settled into a frown. He looked like he wanted to stab her with an eyebrow pencil, but all he said was, "I'm so glad you approve."

Fiona slipped out of the chair, and Linda gestured for me to sit down. "Bernard, Amy is the last model for today."

"And she'll need the most work," Fiona muttered.

"Any special requests?" Bernard asked me, shooting a dark glance at Fiona.

I shook my head. Honestly, I can barely get my lip gloss to go on straight. I figured that a professional stylist didn't need my help. "Whatever you think will look good," I told him.

Bernard actually smiled a little at this, but Fiona rolled her eyes.

"Come on, Fiona," Jenelle said. "Let's go check out our clothes." She tugged at Fiona's hand, pulling her away from the makeup mirror.

"Yeah, like, I've barely even tried anything on?" Lucia said. "I mean, I don't like to wear clothes that aren't *familiar*?"

Bernard set my hair in giant curlers while he worked on my face. His fingers were cold as he dabbed foundation over my forehead, but he had a quick, professional touch, as if he had done this a thousand times before. "How long have you been a makeup artist?" I asked him.

"Twenty-two years," he said, reaching for a tin of silvery eye shadow. "It started as a summer job, believe it or not. Helping do stage makeup in New York City."

"On Broadway?" I asked.

"Off Broadway," he admitted. "But I did eventually do a little work on Broadway. Then I moved on to the world of fashion." He said this last part with a sigh, as if he wasn't quite sure why he'd ever left the theater.

Bernard dabbed some color on my cheeks, lined my eyes, swept on some mascara, and brushed lipstick over my lips. He followed everything with some loose powder. "To set the makeup, so it doesn't come off." Then he added another coat of lipstick and blotted. "No licking your lips," he warned.

I nodded. I do have a bad habit of nibbling my lips when I'm nervous.

Finally, he pulled the rollers out of my hair and brushed it out, then sprayed the whole thing with this stuff that smelled like coconut.

"What do you think?" he asked, holding up a mirror so that I could see the front and back at the same time. Instead of my usual frizz, my hair had morphed into a smooth, bouncy look that was pinned back at the top and loose at the bottom. My skin was practically glowing, and my green eyes looked bright. Bernard had even managed — somehow — to make my too-long nose look good.

"I love it!" I told him. I really did. I mean, this was more makeup than I would ever wear to school. And my hair — although it looked great — had taken almost forty minutes and half a bottle of hair spray to tame. So this wasn't exactly my "everyday look." But I was sure that it would look good under the lights.

"Well, I'm glad *somebody's* happy," Bernard said, checking his watch. "You'd better go change. We've only got about twenty minutes to showtime."

When I hurried over to rack number three, Fiona was standing there, fiddling with a plaid skirt. "Hey, Fiona," I said.

Fiona jumped and wheeled around suddenly to face me. "Oh, hi!" She pursed her lips.

Don't mess up your lipstick, I thought. "Um, I think this is my rack. I'm pretty sure I'm model number three."

"Oh," Fiona said slowly. "Oh — really? Is this rack three?"

I pointed to the large number three taped to the rack.

"Right! Oops! I'm number five." She backed away from the clothes, then scurried over to her rack. She pulled a black jacket off a hanger and ducked into her dressing room.

Okay, that was weird, I thought as I flipped through the clothes. There were four outfits grouped together. *And this is even weirder*, I thought as I held up the first outfit. Yellow-and-brown plaid skirt with orange-and-red-polka-dot shirt. Yellow tights. Brown boots. I hesitated. *Is this right?* The next outfit was slightly more normal. Red sweater and a zebra-print skirt. But with leopard-print shoes, cheetah scarf, and giraffe-print tights it seemed like a bit . . . much. Plus, that outfit came with ropes and ropes of chunky gold jewelry. The other two outfits were equally strange. One was plaid-on-plaid, the other was All Things Aqua. *Am I seriously supposed to wear this?* I wondered what Lucia thought of her outfits — if they were *familiar* enough. Because mine looked like they'd been put together by someone wearing a blindfold.

Looking around, I spotted Jenelle helping a girl with long auburn hair zip up her dress. "Hey, Jenelle," I said. "I just looked at my rack, and the outfits seem a little . . . strange. . . ."

The girl with auburn hair blew out a breath that made her bangs flutter. "Oh, ugh, you should have seen the clothes at the *last* show I did," she said. "Everything was neon. I swear, I thought they were going to turn out the lights and let us glow in the dark."

"Amy, this is Sasha," Jenelle said quickly. "You

49

don't have a safety pin, by any chance, do you? This zipper won't close."

"Um, probably," I admitted. I tend to carry a ton of stuff in my bag. "But these clothes seem like maybe they're mismatched," I said as I fished around at the bottom of my purse. "I don't know if that's the style, or —"

"Look at these shoes!" Sasha said, kicking out a foot with a blue suede heel. "Do you think this goes with a yellow dress?" she demanded, gesturing to her torso.

"But your dress has a blue hem, and — oh, here you go." I pulled a safety pin out of the front pocket of my bag.

"Amy, you're a lifesaver — as usual," Jenelle said, taking the pin. "Don't worry about the clothes. Fashion shows aren't exactly about the kind of outfits you wear on the street — they're meant to inspire you. To get you thinking about clothes. Then people buy the pieces separately. Now go get dressed. We've only got a few minutes!"

"Really?" I cast a doubtful glance at my rack. Maybe Jenelle had a point. "It's just —"

"Don't worry," Jenelle said with a smile. "They're just clothes. Now get going, or you won't make it to the catwalk!"

I smiled back. "Okay," I said. I hurried over to the rack, pulled down the first outfit, then went to my dressing room to change. Just as I was pulling on my boots, the music started pulsing and I heard Eva begin the show. The minute I stepped out of the dressing room, Fiona grabbed my arm. "What's taking so long?" she hissed in my ear as she dragged me toward the curtain. "You're next!"

The next thing I knew, she shoved me forward and I stumbled out onto the catwalk. I saw Sasha walking toward me in her yellow dress. Beyond her, the store was packed. Every seat was full, and people were even standing in the aisles. I spotted my mother standing near the door behind rows and rows of Allington students.

A cold chill passed over my body. I hadn't realized that people I knew would be at the fashion show! *Oh, look,* I thought as I stood there. *It's Voe Silk. And Swoozie Lansing from Spanish class. And Hannah Jakobsen....* My brain was filled with a black void. *What am I supposed to do again?* I thought dimly. Words scattered through my brain. *Fashion frown, blank look, catwalk strut, right, left, pivot, catwalk, blank, frown, pivot, left...*

"Move!" Fiona growled behind me, and I felt a hand shove the exact center of my back. I took a step forward, then another. And then, before I knew it, I was walking down the catwalk. I plastered a huge smile on my face. I wasn't doing anything that Jenelle had taught me, though. I couldn't remember any of it, even though I'd been practicing for twenty-four hours! It was all I could do to walk in a reasonably straight line and not fall over.

"Um, and now we have Amy," Eva said from her spot behind the podium. She was blinking rapidly, as if she was surprised to see me. "She's wearing a blouse by . . . um, Savannah Acton, and a skirt by . . ." Her words drifted over me, like water over stones. *Don't think of "Walking on Sunshine,"* I commanded myself, but — of course — that song immediately started playing in my head, even though something clubby and electronic was pulsing over the speakers.

Halfway down the catwalk, I passed Sasha, whose eyes widened slightly at my outfit. But I didn't even think about it. I just walked to the end, paused, and turned back, trying to ignore the guy with the ponytail, who was taking about fifty photos per second. Other photographers had joined him, and flashbulbs kept popping in my eyes, leaving me half blind.

Finally, finally, the long walk was over. Once I was backstage again, I darted back to my dressing room and changed into the next outfit. *That wasn't so bad*, I thought, even though I was a little worried that my walk had been too bouncy. *Oh, whatever*, I thought as I yanked on some tights. *I survived it, right?*

I walked down the catwalk three more times in different outfits, and before I knew it, the show was over. I breathed a huge sigh of relief as I changed back into my soft pink T-shirt and favorite jeans. It felt funny to have on a face full of makeup with that outfit.

When I stepped out of my dressing room, I found myself face-to-face with Linda. That is — she looked like Linda, only a lot paler and kind of shell-shocked. Jenelle was standing with her, looking wide-eyed and concerned.

When she saw me, Linda placed a hand over her chest. "What *happened*?" she breathed, her voice a half gasp.

My throat went dry as all of the relief I'd felt evaporated. *This is way worse than I thought.* "I'm so sorry," I said quickly. "I tried not to think of 'Walking on Sunshine,' but it just kept —"

"What?" Linda asked. "No, not that — sweetheart, what happened to your *clothes*? Nothing matched! Everything was mixed up!"

"I — what?"

Linda ran a hand through her blond hair. "Oh, this is *terrible*," she wailed. She looked down at her clipboard. "I thought I'd been so careful arranging the outfits. I don't know what could have happened!"

"I'm so sorry, I didn't know —"

"Amy even tried to tell me," Jenelle said miserably. "But I didn't listen. Oh, Mom, this is all my fault."

"It's no one's fault, sweetheart," Linda said. "I'm just worried about what this will do to business —" She put a hand over her mouth, unable to finish. "This is the kind of mix-up that can ruin you."

Suddenly, an image popped into my brain. Fiona, standing near my dressing room, touching my clothes. I looked around. There she was, standing near the curtain with Lucia. She must have felt my eyes on her, because she turned her head to look at me. And then she *smirked*.

I felt the rage wash over me like hot lava — my skin was on fire. *How could she do that?* I thought. But I knew the answer. Fiona had wanted to embarrass me, and now she'd gotten her chance.

I felt my cheeks burn. I'd looked like an idiot in front of half of Allington Academy. And I'd made

Linda and Jenelle look like fools. "I'm so sorry," I whispered.

"Oh, Amy, it's —"

But I didn't stay to listen to what Jenelle had to say. I just hurried toward the back door, wanting to get as far away from Bounce as possible.

As far away from *Fiona* as possible.

"Crickets have no ears. Through what part of their body do they hear?"

I heard Kiwi's voice dimly, as if it was traveling from far away. The question didn't really penetrate my brain until Mitchie poked me in the arm.

"Wake up," she said playfully. "Are you Amy Flowers, or her zombie twin?"

"Hm? What? Sorry." Sighing, I flopped my head against the back of the comfy brown leather couch we were sitting on.

Allington Academy has a café that opens an hour before school starts. You can get cereal there, or delicious scones, fresh fruit salad, bagels, even eggs and English muffins. They also have a huge selection of herbal tea. But even if you aren't hungry, it's a great place to hang out and study a bit or just chat before the bell rings. Mitchie and Kiwi are there most mornings, and if my bus gets in early enough, I join them.

"You've been a little spacey," Kiwi said, reaching for her mug of chai tea. She always brings her own mug — it's a beautiful greenish-blue color, handmade by her aunt. "Is everything okay?"

I sighed. "Still thinking about the fashion show yesterday," I admitted.

Kiwi nodded sympathetically and Mitchie let out a grunt. I'd told them about the disastrous spectacle I'd made of myself on the catwalk. It had haunted me all night. I'd had trouble getting to sleep, and when I did, I had nightmares about walking around in public wearing a garbage bag and a bucket on my head.

"I just feel like such an idiot," I said.

"Fiona's the one who should feel like an idiot," Kiwi said. "I can't believe she did that to her so-called best friend's mother."

"If it's evil, Fiona will do it." Mitchie didn't look up from the pile of flash cards she was flipping through. "She can't help it. She's like a spider. Or a vampire bat or something."

"There were a ton of Allington people there," I confessed. *Maybe they didn't recognize me*, I thought hopefully. *Maybe my awful outfits were too blinding. . . .*

"I'm sure it wasn't as bad as you think," Kiwi said. I knew that she was trying to be nice. But I also knew that it was *at least* as bad as I thought, if not worse.

"Don't worry about it." Mitchie patted my shoulder. "It's not like fashion is your future career or anything."

I forced myself to nod, but I was wincing inside. Honestly, I love to sew and put together outfits. And sometimes, I *do* think that fashion would make a good career for me. But I couldn't say that to Mitchie. She'd just think it was dumb.

"Amy!" called a voice, and I looked up to see Jenelle waving at me frantically as she ran down the hall toward the café. She was out of breath by the time she reached us, and her book bag was falling off her shoulder. She hiked it up and said, "Amy, guess what?" She was smiling, which was kind of a surprise.

"A house finally landed on Fiona?" Mitchie asked hopefully. "The Munchkins are thrilled?"

Jenelle shot her a Look, then turned back to me. "You'll never believe it, but the crowd went completely berserk after the show. We sold more in a day than we usually do in a week. Mom said it was the most successful fashion show ever!"

I felt my chin drop practically to my chest. "You're *kidding*."

Kiwi touched her toe to my ankle. "I told you that you didn't do as badly as you thought."

"Not *bad*?" Jenelle repeated. Her hazel eyes were huge. "Amy, almost everything we sold was the stuff *you* were wearing!"

At that moment, a group of five sixth-grade girls walked past our couch. One of them was wearing the polka-dot shirt with a striped skirt, another had on a crazy array of animal prints, and a third was wearing mismatched plaid. The one in the plaid — a pretty South Asian girl with gleaming dark hair and long legs — whispered something to the group, and they all looked over at me. Then they burst into giggles and shuffled off down the hall.

"See?" Jenelle said, jutting her chin toward the backs of the retreating sixth graders. "We sold out of that polka-dot shirt, and we're on back order for the plaids. And look!" She flipped open her messenger bag and pulled out a few copies of a slim, glossy magazine. It was the latest issue of the *Allington Observer*. Jenelle flipped it open to page four. Her peach nail hovered above a photo of me walking down the catwalk in the crazy animal-print outfit. "Hot off the press," Jenelle said with a smile as she sat down on the arm of the couch. "I'm friends with Lali Wood, the fashion writer. She gave me the first copy."

I read the caption out loud. "'Amy Flowers shines at the Bounce fashion show as she models the new Eclectic Chic look.'"

Mitchie and Kiwi leaned in to peer at the article. "What's 'eclectic'?" Kiwi asked.

"It sort of means a combination of a lot of weird stuff," Mitchie explained. "Well, that's certainly accurate."

"The article says that you were the only model bold enough to pull off Bounce's new signature look," Kiwi said. She looked up at me, beaming. "Awesome!"

"Who's that?" Mitchie asked, pointing to a photo of a black-haired girl in a black dress.

Jenelle cocked her head and looked at the picture. "It's Fiona," she said.

"Why is she so pale?" Mitchie asked. "She looks like an extra from a vampire movie."

Jenelle didn't reply, although, of course, I knew the answer. *Fiona should have listened to Bernard*, I thought.

"Listen, Amy," Jenelle said, tucking the extra magazines back into her bag, "Bounce is sponsoring a fund-raiser right here at Allington. It's another fashion show, only this time, we're raising money for the library. Mom was hoping that you would help with some of the planning. And some of the styling."

"She wants me to help plan outfits?" I asked.

"Why not? She says you have a natural feel for it, given that you pulled off some of the most outrageous looks ever seen on a runway." Jenelle fiddled nervously with a button on her pale pink short-sleeved cardigan. But I noticed that even she was wearing a pink plaid skirt and brown plaid tights. *It looks like everyone is into the new look*, I thought. "It's in two weeks," Jenelle continued. "We're going to pick the models tomorrow after school. Can you help?"

"Sure," I said, feeling a warm smile spread across my face. "I'd love to!"

"Great! Okay, I'll see you later then! I can't wait to show Lucia and Fiona the article!" Jenelle clapped her hands in excitement. "This is going to be so much fun!" She waved, then turned and bounced away.

"Fun?" Mitchie repeated. Her right eyebrow was arched. "I hope so."

"Why?" I asked. "Don't you think it sounds fun?"

Mitchie flipped the flash cards absently — *ziiip, ziiip.* "Well . . ." she said at last. "The League ran the same fund-raiser last year. Which means, of course, that Fiona was in charge." She gave me a sideways glance. "I don't know how happy she'll be about having help."

A cold chill settled into my chest. *I'm going to have to work with Fiona?* I hadn't really counted on that. . . . I was just about to say something like, "Do you think I should try to get out of it?" when Preston Harringford walked up.

His mouth was open — to make some sarcastic remark, no doubt — when his eye fell on the magazine in my lap. It was still open to the page with the photos of the fashion show. "What's this?" he asked, plucking it from me before I could swat his hand away. "Oh, my." His eyes traveled from the photo to me, then back to the photo. Finally, he just cracked up. "Looking *good*," he said sarcastically, tossing the magazine back to me.

"Who asked you?" I demanded, but he was already walking away, laughing his head off. "I can't believe I have to put up with that guy," I muttered.

"I guess it's the price of fame," Kiwi said seriously, blowing across the top of her hot tea.

I sighed. So far, everything about this fashion show was *way* more than I had bargained for.

CHAPTER FOUR

Out: Study guides
In: Study dates

"Hey," Scott said just as I was reaching for a white-chocolate macadamia-nut cookie. "Aren't those the best?" He smiled down at me, and I felt as warm and melty as the just-baked cookie on my plate.

"Delicious," I said. My voice sounded a little breathless and dreamy . . . but I couldn't help it. Scott was standing right next to me with the clean smell of laundry detergent wafting up from his blue Rice University T-shirt. It had a picture of an owl, Rice's mascot, over his heart.

"I think I'll grab one, too," he said, reaching for a small plate. His hand brushed mine for a moment.

As I watched him place the plate on his tray and stick his hand in the front pocket of his jeans, I could still feel the warm spot on my finger where our hands had briefly met. "So, you know that there's another meeting tonight, right? Team study?"

"Hm?" His big brown eyes were staring down at me, and I realized that he was waiting for an answer. The question finally made its way through my skull, as if it had traveled there from another time zone. "Oh, right," I said quickly. "We're meeting at Zach's." That was a local bagel place.

Scott nodded. "So . . ." He shifted his weight from one leg to the other.

"So . . ." I wracked my brain for something to say. *If you don't say anything, he'll just walk off*, my mind warned.

"Excuse me," said a tall, muscular guy with a crew cut. "You guys are blocking the cookies."

"Sorry!" I jumped back a little to give him room. Scott grabbed his tray and we both headed for the exit. "Where are you sitting?"

"The Fern Room," Scott replied. "My friends and I are usually in there or in Orchid."

"Orchid? Isn't that a little girly?" I teased. The Orchid Room is done all in pink and purple.

Scott shrugged. "It's the closest room to the entrance, and my friends are incredibly lazy."

I laughed.

"Um, listen, I was just wondering if you ever . . . you know . . ." He shifted his tray to balance on one arm and raked his fingers through his soft-looking sandy-blond hair. ". . . if you ever wanted to get together sometime. To study."

"I — sure —" I cocked my head. "Aren't we doing that tonight?"

"I mean just the two of us," Scott added quickly. "You know, the group is great and everything, but you can get a lot more done with just a couple of people."

"Oh, absolutely." I nodded to show how serious I was about accomplishing as much during our study session as possible. *He doesn't have to know that my heart is playing hopscotch through my stomach right now*, I thought. *And he also doesn't need to know that I'd happily get together with him to do anything — including visit the dentist or take my dog to be dewormed.*

"I was thinking Saturday?" Scott suggested. "Maybe around eleven, at the library?"

"Perfect!" I told him. *It really is perfect*, I thought. *That way, we can study for a while, then maybe take a break, have lunch. . . .*

64

"Really? I mean — great."

I nodded. "Great."

"Great," he repeated.

We stood there a minute, just smiling, and I wondered if we'd ever think of anything besides "great" to say to each other. I certainly couldn't think of any other word. *Greatgreatgreatgreatgreat!* My brain kept repeating it on an endless loop. *This is so* great*!*

"Okay, well . . ." Scott jerked his thumb over his shoulder. "I guess I'd better go join my friends."

"See you later," I told him.

"Definitely." He flashed me a final smile over his shoulder before he disappeared through the green doorway to the Fern Room.

I headed across the hall to the butter-yellow Sunflower door.

"What are you so smiley about?" Kiwi asked as I plunked my tray down across from Mitchie.

"Oh, nothing. . . ." I singsonged. *I have a date with Scott!* I thought as I plucked a potato chip from my plate and popped it into my mouth.

"Then why are you humming?" Kiwi pressed.

"I wasn't humming."

Kiwi looked at Mitchie.

"You were humming," she confirmed. "You're humming right now."

I actually hadn't realized that I was humming until that moment. It was that stupid "Walking on Sunshine" song again. *Why can't I get you out of my head?* I thought as the song played on.

Kiwi took a sip of her cranberry drink and eyed me coolly. It was obvious that she knew something was up.

"Okay — it's just — I ran into Scott, and he asked if I wanted to study this weekend," I confessed. I could feel myself blushing a little as I said it.

"Oooh!" Kiwi's eyes were round. "That's so awesome!"

"Absolutely," Mitchie agreed. "We need all of the study time we can get! What time are we meeting?" She pulled a little notebook out of her bag and flipped it open.

Kiwi and I stared at her a moment, then exchanged glances.

"What?" Mitchie asked. "We're going to study for the Challenge, right?"

"Um . . . well . . ." I felt my blush turn even hotter and shifted in my seat. *How can I let Mitchie know that she isn't invited?* I wondered.

"Mitchie, Amy and Scott have a study *date*." Kiwi emphasized the word "date," and I resisted

66

the urge to insist that it wasn't a date. *After all, if it isn't a date, then why can't Mitchie come along?*

Mitchie looked blank for a moment. Then, all of a sudden, her dark eyebrows lifted slightly. "Oh," she said slowly. "Ohhhh."

"It's — it's not like you're not invited," I said lamely. "It's just —"

Mitchie held up a hand. "I get it," she said, flipping her notebook closed. "No problem."

Suddenly, I felt really bad. Like I was excluding Mitchie on purpose or something. But I hadn't meant to. . . . I felt torn. Part of me wanted to insist that Mitchie come along. And another part of me knew that was completely *nuts.*

"Amy's going to the library with a cute boy," Kiwi teased, her eyes sparkling. "They're going to *study.*"

A slow grin spread up the side of Mitchie's face. "They need some alone time," she put in. "They have a lot of *research* to do."

She and Kiwi dissolved into giggles, and so did I.

"You know," Kiwi went on in a mock-serious tone, "it's very important to plan your outfit for a study date. The wrong thing can really mess up your concentration." She flipped her long auburn hair over one shoulder.

"Maybe that's what Amy's going for," Mitchie suggested, and we all cracked up.

"So tell us," Kiwi said, shoving aside Mitchie's huge pile of books. "What were you thinking?"

Honestly, I was barely managing to think anything other than *greatgreatgreatgreatgreat!* again. Planning a wardrobe seemed like the kind of thing people were doing in a parallel universe. Then again, talking about it would give me an excuse to talk about Scott some more. . . .

And I didn't mind that at all.

"Do you mind if I take your photo, Shannon?" Jenelle asked the girl sitting in front of us. She held up a small silver digital camera. "We're taking photos of everyone who's trying out."

"Oh, no problem," Shannon said as Fiona let out a sigh.

"Don't waste your time," Fiona muttered as Jenelle pressed the button.

"Well, thanks for coming in," Jenelle said. "We're going to post the names of the models tomorrow morning, so you can check the list on the main kiosk at the entrance."

"Okay," Shannon said. She smiled shyly at us and ducked out the door.

"You might want to bring a magnifying

glass," Fiona said snarkily as the door swung shut. "Because you'll have to look *real* hard to find your name."

"What was wrong with her?" I asked.

"Oh, please." Fiona rolled her eyes. "We're selling clothes, not perfume."

What? I glanced at Jenelle, who gave me an "I have no idea" shrug. "What does that mean?"

"It means, like, she had an enormous nose?" Lucia explained. "It took up half her face?"

I sighed. So far, we'd seen fifteen possible models, and Fiona had managed to make a mean comment about almost every one of them. I guess she thought that nobody was good enough to be in the Fashion Fund-raiser but her and the rest of the League.

"Next," Fiona shouted, placing a big, fat X mark at the top of Shannon's form, right over her name and contact info.

A girl with long, straight, white-blond hair and huge blue eyes appeared. She walked slowly into the room, almost as if she wasn't really sure where she was. "Hi," she said. She handed her form to Jenelle, and Fiona leaned over to take a look at it.

"Hi, Pear." Jenelle motioned for Pear to have a seat. "So, tell us, why are you interested in modeling for the Fashion Fund-raiser?" This was something we were asking everyone — it was supposed to break the ice a little and help us get to know the models who were auditioning.

Pear looked blank, and she didn't say anything for a long time. Just as I was tempted to give her a poke in the arm to make sure that she was still awake, she blinked twice and cleared her throat. "I guess because . . . I like . . . clothes."

Jenelle waited a moment to see if Pear was going to add anything. She didn't. "Okay," Jenelle said brightly. "Why don't you walk for us? Just to the door and back."

Pear stood up and shuffled to the door. She had a weird, slouchy way of walking — her hips seemed to arrive everywhere six inches before the rest of her body. *This girl is a definite no*, I thought as I watched her do the step, pivot, turn, step, and slouch back toward us.

Then Jenelle took her photo and told her to check for her name the next day.

"Okay," Pear said in her blank way. Then she walked through the door — which, I realized, had about as much personality as she did. I turned to Fiona, waiting to hear her comment. I was sure it would be good.

"She's in," Fiona said.

"Definitely?" Lucia agreed. "I loved her hair?"

"And her skin," Fiona agreed.

"What?" My voice had a definite screechy quality, but I couldn't help it. "Are you guys serious?"

Fiona looked at me coolly. "Absolutely. Pear Waters is one of the most beautiful girls in the school — everyone knows that."

"Don't you think she's pretty?" Lucia asked. Her delicate brown eyebrows drew together, as if she couldn't understand why I wouldn't want Pear in the show.

"Well . . . yes," I admitted. "She's pretty. But she's got about as much personality as a . . . well . . . as a pear!"

"What does personality have to do with anything?" Fiona demanded. "We're looking for models, not running the Miss Congeniality pageant."

"I thought that Linda wanted the show to be fun," I countered. "I thought that the whole idea was to make the clothes seem cool." I looked over at Jenelle.

"That's true," she admitted.

Lucia looked down at the *Allington Observer*. It was open to the page with the photos from the show. At the start of the audition, Jenelle had showed us a note from her mother. "We have to make this look work!" the Post-it read, with an arrow pointing at my crazy outfit. I could tell Lucia was thinking that over. Pear might be beautiful, but I doubted she could pull off the Eclectic Chic look. And I think Lucia doubted it, too.

Fiona just shook her head and placed a check mark at the top of Pear's form. That meant "Maybe." *Okay,* I thought as Fiona shouted, "Next!" *We'll come back to her later.*

The door swung open. "Hi, guys!" A girl with a round face and sparkling brown eyes bounced in. "How's it going?" She had a big smile that seemed to take over her whole face.

"Great," I said warmly just as Fiona said, "It's going fine."

"Hi, Brooke," Jenelle said as Brooke handed over her form and sat down on the metal folding chair across from us. "I think you know everyone."

"Everyone except Amy." Brooke grinned at me. "Of course, everyone knows who you are — especially after that big photo spread in the *Observer*! Nice to meet you."

"Same," I told her. There was something about Brooke that made me like her right away. And I especially loved her hair — it was a deep shade of auburn and incredibly curly. Unique, like her.

"So, why do you want to be in the Fashion Fund-raiser?" Jenelle asked.

"Well, as you guys know, I'm president of the seventh-grade class," Brooke explained. "And I think it's important to help raise funds for the library. But, also, I think fashion is fun! I've always wanted to do something like this."

I nodded. I hadn't realized that Brooke was class president — those elections were held in the spring for the following year, and I hadn't been a student at Allington last term.

"Great," Jenelle said. "Let's see you walk."

Brooke had a nice, smooth walk, and when she turned, she added a little flair — she swished out her hip, gave us a huge smile, and walked back.

"Okay," Jenelle told her as she snapped her photo. "Thanks! We're posting the list on the kiosk tomorrow morning."

"Excellent!" Brooke said. "This was so great. Good luck with the rest of the auditions!" She waved cheerfully and left.

"Yes, we'll definitely see you later," Fiona said, making a note on Brooke's form. "*Much* later," she added in a mumble.

"Are you serious?" I demanded. "She's perfect!"

"Perfect?" Fiona repeated. "Perfectly round, you mean."

"Yeah," Lucia agreed. "And she has, like, freckles?"

"What?" Okay, so Brooke was a little overweight and she had a light spray of freckles across her nose. So what? That was what made her look unique! "She's pretty! And I'll bet she knows everyone in the seventh grade — the whole class will probably come to the show if she's in it."

"That's true," Jenelle agreed. "She has a ton of friends."

"Besides, she seems totally fun, and that's what we're going for. Right?" I demanded. "She's got the attitude!"

Fiona looked at me coldly. "She's not right for the show."

I didn't back down. "And I say she is."

"Fine," Fiona snapped. "Then let's vote on it. I say no." She tapped Brooke's form with the end of her pen and glowered at me.

"I vote yes," I said.

"I say yes, too," Jenelle put in.

Anger flared in Fiona's eyes, but she didn't say anything. She just turned to Lucia, whose bottom lip puffed out in a glossy pout.

Oh, great, I thought. *We're going to be here all night, locked in a two-to-two tie.*

"Well, I . . ." She looked from me to Fiona, then back to me. "I just . . ." She cleared her throat. "Yes?" she whispered finally.

Surprise burst through me like a tiny spark. *Lucia said yes?*

But I knew it had to be true, because Fiona looked like she was about to strangle something. "All right," she snapped. "Fine." She drew a star at the top of the form. "Next!" she shouted.

A little thrill of triumph shot through me. Brooke was in! *Good — she deserves it,* I thought as I glanced up at the clock on the wall. *Ugh.* I needed to leave in ten minutes to make it to that night's Academic Challenge study session. I bit my lip, casting a glance at Fiona out of the corner of my eye. She was frowning at the girl who had just walked in. I could practically read her thoughts: *Eyebrows too heavy, lower lip too full, face too pale. . . .* Fiona only wanted a certain type for the Fashion Fund-raiser — that is, people who looked like her. She didn't care about personality.

We still had ten slots to fill. Outside the door, the hallway was packed with kids who wanted to try out for the fund-raiser. *If I leave now,* I thought,

Fiona will get to fill the show with her friends and the girls who look "right." She'll shut out the best models. And we'll be stuck with no-personality girls . . . a show full of Pears.

I just couldn't let that happen.

The latest model candidate had just finished explaining her reasons for wanting to be in the show.

"Um, excuse me," I told her. Then I leaned toward Jenelle and whispered, "Could I borrow your cell phone for a minute?" Despite many months of begging, my parents still hadn't agreed to get me a phone. Which was a real pain.

"Sure." Jenelle dug around in her bag and came up with a pale pink phone. She flipped it open and handed it to me.

"I'll just be a sec," I said, heading to the back of the room. I ducked out the rear door. *Wow, the hallway really is packed*, I noticed. Girls were standing against lockers, sitting cross-legged on the floor, playing cards, reading, chatting. Each one of them had a form. *It looks like we could be here another couple of hours.*

I punched in Mitchie's phone number and pressed the phone to my ear.

"Hello?" Mitchie said.

"Hey, Mitchie, it's me," I said. "Amy. Um, listen, I — uh — I can't make it to the study session tonight."

"Everything okay?" There was a slight edge of concern in Mitchie's voice.

"Yeah. Fine. I'm just stuck at school for another couple of hours, I think." I winced a little at the truth that I was leaving out.

But — of course — Mitchie didn't let it go at that. "What's going on at school?" she asked. "Studying for something else?"

"No . . . it's . . ." I nibbled at the inside of my lip. "It's just this Fashion Fund-raiser thing. The try-outs aren't over yet. I can't leave."

Silence.

"Oh," Mitchie said.

Silencesilencesilence.

I wanted to say something, but I wasn't sure what. I knew that if I explained the Fiona situation to Mitchie, she'd just tell me that it wasn't worth it. She'd say that there's no point fighting Fiona — she always gets her way in the end.

But that isn't true, I told myself. *Look at what happened with Brooke!*

"I'll just have to study on my own," I said instead. "Until the next session." At that moment,

77

though, I remembered that I had promised Jenelle I would put together a few sample outfits for the fund-raiser. *So when am I supposed to study for the Challenge?* I had a ton of homework to do, too. *I guess I can wake up early*, I thought.

"Yeah . . ." Mitchie said slowly. "Okay. Well, we'll miss you." The last sentence hung there for a moment, like she wanted to add something. But she didn't.

"See you tomorrow," I said lamely, and then we both hung up.

I flipped the phone closed, feeling a pang of guilt. I knew that the Academic Challenge was really important to Mitchie, and I felt like a jerk for bagging the study session at the last minute. *But I don't have a choice*, I thought, looking at the crowd of girls jammed into the hallway. *Not really.*

Not unless I want to let Fiona have her way.

And I knew for sure that I didn't want to do that. Not this time.

CHAPTER FIVE

In: Kiwis
Out: Pears

I poked my head into the Sunflower Room, hitching my tote higher onto my shoulder with one hand and steadying my tray with the other. *Hm. Still no Kiwi or Mitchie.* I'd waited for them earlier, but neither one had shown up at our usual table. That was weird. They usually got to lunch before me.

Well, I thought, *maybe I should look for Jenelle, instead.* I'd planned to take the last ten minutes of lunch to show her a few of the outfits I'd put together the night before. *But I might as well show her now*, I reasoned. *Since my friends are nowhere in sight.*

I made my way to the deep-maroon Dahlia Room. It was darker than the Sunflower, and much quieter. The League was at their usual table by the enormous window overlooking the golf course. Sunlight leaked in at an angle, glinting off of Fiona's hair as she picked at a small piece of steak, chewing in tiny little nibbles. Fiona always took forever to eat — no wonder, since she ate everything in rabbit bites.

"Hi, everyone," I said as I walked up to the table.

Fiona looked up at me from beneath her dark lashes and just kept chewing. We'd had kind of a rough afternoon the day before. In the end, she had to give in on some of my models, and I had to give in on some of hers. Pear, for example, was in. But so was Ja'Nee Jackson, the funniest girl in our grade, if not the known universe.

"Hey, Amy," Jenelle said warmly, gesturing to the empty seat beside her. I set down my tray and hauled my tote bag onto the table.

"I brought a few outfits," I said, pulling out a brown corduroy jacket with patch pockets and raw edges. I held it up with a narrow denim skirt and a pink striped hoodie. "You wear the hoodie under the jacket," I explained.

Fiona blew a long breath through her nostrils,

dragon-style. "Are you serious?" she demanded. "People will laugh that outfit off the stage."

"I don't know," Jenelle said, touching the jacket gingerly. "I think it's cool. It's — different."

"Yeah, it's different?" Lucia agreed in a sarcastic voice. "The way, like, the ugly duckling was different?"

I resisted the urge to point out that the duckling was *different* because it was a *swan* but instead pulled a pair of sky-blue leggings from the bag. "Okay, what about this?" I suggested. "You wear this green skirt over them, and top it with this wrap shirt."

Fiona let out a scoffing little laugh. "Amy, that outfit is totally —"

"Funky!" said a voice. "Omigosh — I *lerve* this look!" Voe Silk reached out with a manicured hand and grabbed the wrap shirt. She was one of the coolest eighth-grade girls at Allington, and she was standing with two of her best friends, Meena Khan and Leticia Martin. As she held the wrap shirt up against her shoulders, I noticed that her nails were painted a vibrant peacock blue. That was Voe — she was a serious dramarama with her own sense of style. "What do you think?" she asked her friends. "Is it me?"

"Like it came out under your own label!" Meena gushed, pulling a handful of waist-length black hair forward over her shoulder. She played with the ends a bit, adding, "And I just love that hoodie! I'd never have thought to wear it with a jacket."

I beamed as Leticia asked, "What's with the fashion show? What are all of these clothes doing here during lunch?"

"We're putting together the Fashion Fundraiser," I explained.

"Oh, right, I saw the signs for the tryouts," Voe said as she reached for the leggings. "These are so soft! Feel them!"

Meena and Leticia reached out and stroked the fabric. "Oooh," Meena said. "Velvety."

"These clothes are so cool," Voe said to Fiona. "And so not like the boring stuff you usually see. You guys are fashion geniuses!"

"Uh, thanks," Fiona said.

"Check these out," I said, pulling a pair of flats from my bag. They were heavily embroidered, beaded with orange flowers and green leaves.

"*Lerve* them!" Meena squealed.

"What does 'lerve' mean?" Jenelle asked.

"Oh, it's just this word we made up. It means that you *love* them," Leticia explained, "and that you *deserve* them. Anything you've just gotta have!"

"Listen," Voe said as she slipped into the seat beside Fiona, "I know we're too late to try out to be models, but do you think maybe we could be ushers? We could, you know, wear some of these outfits while we show people to their seats."

"Extra advertising," Leticia said as she studied a patchwork denim skirt. "I call this!"

"Oh —" Fiona cast a sideways glance at Jenelle, who nodded eagerly, round-eyed. "Yes, absolutely!"

"Great! I can hardly wait to see what else you fashionistas come up with!" Voe placed the leggings back on the table.

"I don't want to let go of these," Meena said. She was still holding the beaded shoes.

"I'll make sure you get to wear them at the show," I promised her.

"Really?" Reluctantly, she handed them over. "Do you need to write my name down or something? It's spelled M-E-E —"

"I'll remember," I promised her.

With a gush of excited whispers, Voe and her friends made their way to their usual table at the other end of the room.

"This is, like, the greatest thing ever?" Lucia said the moment they were out of earshot. "We've never had eighth graders come to the show before?"

"Voe even has friends in high school," Fiona pointed out. "Some of them may come now, too." She skimmed her eyes over the pile of clothes beside me. "So . . . uh . . . Amy . . . are you going to put together a few more combinations?"

"I'll work on it," I told her. I tried really hard not to gloat. It wasn't easy, though.

"My mom has a new shipment coming in this afternoon," Jenelle said. "I'll drop the stuff by your house later."

"Sounds great," I told her as I gathered my things. The bell was just about to ring, and I wanted to eat at least a little of my brown rice and veggie salad. But I wasn't sure that I wanted to do it at Fiona's table.

I made my way back to the Sunflower Room and found Mitchie at our usual spot.

"Hey! There you are!" I said as I sat down across from her. "I didn't see you at the beginning of lunch."

Mitchie finished chewing her turkey wrap. "I was at the library," she explained. "With the team.

We just dashed back here for the last ten minutes to grab something to eat."

"You were?" I paused, a fork of rice and grilled veggies halfway to my lips. "Did I know we had a meeting?"

"We just decided last night to get together," Mitchie said. "I sent you an e-mail."

"Oh."

She smiled apologetically. "Sorry."

"No, I — it's just — I didn't get it." To tell the truth, I hadn't had a chance to check my e-mail at all the night before. The moment I'd gotten home, I had to eat dinner, then put together the fund-raiser outfits, then finish an English essay, twenty math problems, and read two chapters in my history book. I'd crashed into bed a half hour later than usual, dead tired, and woke up late. So late that I missed the bus and didn't get a chance to chat with my friends before school. "Sorry I missed the session."

Mitchie took another bite of her wrap and chewed silently for a moment. "I was just wondering. . . . You know, the first round of the Challenge is a week from Saturday. Are you — do you think you'll be ready?"

"Definitely," I said.

"Because Arielle has offered to sub in." Mitchie said it as if she wasn't very eager to see Arielle take my spot.

I wasn't very eager to see that happen, either. "No, no," I said quickly. "I've missed the sessions, but I've been studying on my own." After all, I'd had a little time to study while my dad drove me to school that morning. Of course, I'd been so tired that my eyes kept closing as I tried to read the flash cards. *I must have absorbed* something, I reasoned. Besides, I still had a few days to cram.

"Great," Mitchie said with a smile. "I know Arielle's really smart and everything — but I'd rather have you on the team."

"I'll be ready," I promised.

I hoped it was true.

"Hey," Scott said as I plopped my book bag onto the library table and slid into the seat across from his. He was at the table right in front of the huge wall of windows. Sunlight streamed in, backlighting his sandy hair. He looked like he was outlined in gold. "I was starting to wonder if you'd forgotten."

"Not possible," I told him, pulling a notebook from my bag. I took a deep breath, willing my heart to settle down. It wasn't easy — not with

Scott sitting right there, looking up at me with big brown eyes. "Mom got a call just as we were leaving the house," I explained. "Sorry I'm late." As the words left my lips, I wondered how many times I'd uttered them in the past week. *More than in the rest of my life combined*, I guessed. I was starting to get sick of saying them — even though, this time, it really *wasn't* my fault.

"No big deal," Scott said. "So, what do you want to do first? And please don't say word problems." He opened his eyes wide in mock horror. "If I have to calculate for one more value of X . . ." He let the sentence dangle.

"Right. One more word problem, and you're over the edge," I told him. "Got it."

"At least let me take a break for forty-five minutes," he begged.

"I probably need more help than you do, anyway," I told him. "I'm the one who's been missing all of the study sessions."

"No problem." Scott reached for a stack of laminated index cards. "Want me to quiz you?"

"Sure," I told him.

"What do you want to start with?" he asked.

I hesitated, unsure whether I should go for a topic I didn't know well or one I was pretty confident about. If I went for one I didn't know well, I'd get more out of the study session . . . but I'd risk looking like an idiot. I decided to go with something I'd studied. "How about space?" I suggested.

"Okay." He flipped to the purple flash cards and pulled one out. "What's the hottest planet in the solar system?" he asked.

"Mercury," I replied.

Scott flipped over the card. "Actually," he said, "it's Venus."

"It is?" I bit my lip. *Embarrassing.* "But Mercury is closest to the sun."

Scott shrugged. "I guess that's what they're counting on you to think."

I was really starting to regret having missed so many sessions.

"Okay, here's another." Scott flipped to the next card. "How many times has Neptune been around the sun since its discovery in 1846?"

Hmm . . . Neptune is the planet farthest from the sun, not counting Pluto, which some people don't even think is a planet anymore. So it would take a seriously long time for it to orbit. . . . Still, I had no idea. "Less than fifty?" I asked.

"Much less."

Thirty? Fifteen? I had no idea, and I didn't want to just start spouting numbers. *A great way to look non-brilliant.* "Give me a hint," I begged.

Scott paused to look at the back of the card. "It's either twenty-three, seventeen, eight, or zero," he said.

"Seventeen?" I asked weakly. Scott started to shake his head, so I changed my answer. "Twenty-three?"

"It's zero," Scott said. "It's only gone about seventy-five percent of the way." He looked at me a moment, then moved on. "What's the difference between a meteoroid and a meteorite?"

Finally! Something I'd studied! I answered reflexively, without pausing to think. "A meteoroid is what the rock is called when it falls to earth, and a meteorite is what it's called when it's in space." I leaned back in my chair, feeling both relieved and proud.

But Scott frowned. "Actually, a meteoroid is what it's called in space."

"That's what I said," I told him.

"You said the opposite."

"I did?"

Scott nodded.

At this point, I started wishing that a meteor would come crashing through the roof of the library and put me out of my misery. Scott was giving me this Look — like he felt really sorry for me. *Humiliating.* I wanted to yank my backpack over my head and hide. "Look, Scott, I — I'm usually much better than this," I babbled. "I don't know what's wrong with my brain right now. . . ." *Except for the fact that you've barely had time to study*, said one part of my brain.

Oh, be quiet, said the other part. *Can't you see I'm doing the best I can?*

And just when I thought things couldn't get worse, they did.

"Hey, guys!" Preston said as he dropped into the seat beside me. "What's going on? A mini Challenge study group?"

I stared at him for a minute. *What is he doing here?* I wondered. *And how can I get him to leave?*

"We're just going over some science questions," Scott explained.

"Right," I butted in. "So if you don't mind —"

"Hey, what's this?" Preston asked, reaching for something on the table. My oversized purse had flopped over, and a small cylinder had fallen out. "You carry around a mini-flashlight?" Preston clicked it on, shining it in my eyes. "Why?"

"Give me that," I said, grabbing at the light. "You never know when you might need it."

"You mean, like, if you fall into a well or something?" Preston teased. "What else have you got in here?" He dragged my purse into his lap. I tried to grab it away from him, but he yanked it out of my reach. "Oh, look — a pencil sharpener in the shape of a frog!" He passed the green plastic sharpener to Scott, who laughed.

"Wow, Amy, you certainly are *prepared*," Preston said as he dug a tiny travel toothbrush from my bag.

"You're supposed to brush after every meal," I shot back.

"And you actually *do* it?" Preston pulled out a half-squeezed-out tube of toothpaste. "Guess so. What other goodies do you have? Ooh! An ancient fun-sized Almond Joy left over from Halloween! Look — it's practically a fossil." He banged the rock-hard candy against the library table.

Scott was really cracking up now, and I half dove over the table to snatch my bag from Preston's hands. "Cut it out," I growled, yanking it away from him.

"Okay, okay." Holding up his hands, Preston gave me a wicked grin. "But, hey, that candy bar made me hungry. Anyone else hungry? How 'bout we move this study party over to Daily Blend?"

I was shaking my head no, but Preston was looking at Scott, who said, "Sure. We aren't really getting much done here, anyway."

I grimaced. *Ouch.* "But shouldn't we — don't we need to study?"

"We can still study," Preston insisted. "But it'll be better if we get something to eat first."

Who is "we"? I thought as I glared at him. *You keep saying "we" as if someone invited you to join us!* But I didn't say that out loud because — apparently — Scott was thinking of Preston as part of "we." He was already packing up his books, snapping a rubber band around the flash cards, and tucking them into his olive-drab messenger bag.

Grr. I fumed silently as we walked over to Daily Blend, which is only a block from the Allington campus. It turns out that Preston and Scott were both on the soccer team — they spent the whole walk chatting about their game the week before and some "totally amazing" goal that Preston had scored. It was "totally amazing" according to Preston, of course. *What is the most annoying thing in the universe?* I mused sarcastically. *A Prestonoid or a Prestonite?*

Okay, maybe we can ditch him after lunch, I thought as I tagged along behind them. *I'll just say that we need to get more studying done, and I need a quiet place, like the library, to study. . . . After all, he can't hang out with us forever. He'll have to go home* sometime.

I hope.

I tried to shake off my annoyance as we walked up to Daily Blend. They mostly serve coffee drinks (bleucch) and smoothies (yum), but they also have awesome sandwiches on homemade bread. They must have been baking some at that moment, because the most delicious smell in the world wafted over us as we opened the door.

"Something smells great," Scott said as we stepped inside.

"I'll bet it's coming from the bottom of Amy's bag," Preston joked as he scanned the restaurant for a table.

I rolled my eyes. "Ha-ha."

"Hey, look!" Preston said. "It's the rest of our posse!"

Sure enough, Mitchie and Arielle were sitting in a corner booth.

"Let's join them!" And before I could even take a breath, he had started across the floor toward them.

Arielle had her back to us as we walked toward their table. "Not only that, there are a hundred and seventeen elements on the table, the most abundant element in the universe is hydrogen, and the only letter in the alphabet that isn't on the periodic table is *J*—"

"Hey! Studying hard?" Preston asked as he slid into the booth beside Mitchie. "How's it going? Man, Mitchie, you're a total machine. Do you ever stop? I'm serious, I think you've got gears in your skull instead of brains. Hey, Arielle. How's the Speed Spout Method?"

"I think it's working." Arielle looked smug.

I wondered vaguely what the Speed Spout Method was, but decided that I didn't care enough to ask because Mitchie was — at that moment — looking from me to Scott to Preston wearing a "What's this?" look. Her eyes landed back on mine, and I shook my head slightly and sort of waved my hand in Preston's direction in an attempt to communicate that he'd just barged in on our study session uninvited. But Mitchie simply cocked her head in confusion as Scott sat down beside Arielle. I continued to stand there. I guess I just couldn't accept that this was really happening — my date with Scott was officially going nowhere.

"What are you eating?" Preston asked Arielle. "That looks great."

"Avocado and cheese sandwich," Arielle said. "And by the way, avocados are a fruit, not a vegetable. Genus: *Persea*. Family: Lauraceae."

"Avocado fun facts." Preston nodded seriously. He flashed me a small grin as he pulled menus from the rack behind the napkins and handed them out. "I'm starved! This is great — we'll get a bite, and then we can all study together for the rest of the afternoon!" Preston grinned at me, his perfectly even white teeth gleaming.

"Perfect," I said without enthusiasm as I finally gave up and sat down. I sneaked a glance at Scott, but he was absorbed in the menu. Lovely. I'd looked like an idiot in front of him, and now our twosome had become a fivesome. How cozy.

File this day under Worst Non-date Ever.

Flwrpwr: You there?

I tapped the edge of my keyboard as I waited for Mitchie to reply. Her name was on my buddy list, so I figured she was on the computer . . . unless she was like my brother, who always forgets to log off. But her reply came almost instantly:

Sk8rgrrrl: Hey.

Flwrpwr: Studying?

Sk8rgrrrl: Taking a break. Akina just made peach muffins. ☺

I drew in a deep breath, my fingers poised lightly on the keys. It was Sunday evening, and I was still feeling bad about the day before. I'd never had a chance to explain that Preston had just barged in on my non-date with Scott. But now, typing all of that up via chat seemed too hard — like I'd just make a bigger mess of the situation. So instead I typed, "Can you talk?"

Sk8rgrrrl: Sure. Call me.

I darted upstairs and grabbed the cordless from my side table, then flopped on my bed as I punched in the number. Mitchie answered in one ring.

"My brain hurts," she griped.

"That's what happens when you cram too much information inside," I joked.

"Tell it to Arielle," Mitchie shot back. "That stupid Speed Spout Method is going to drive me crazy."

"Yeah, what's the deal?" I asked. Something was poking me in the shoulder. Reaching behind my back, I pulled a green sweater on a hanger that had somehow gotten lodged between my pillows. Not surprising, given that my room kind of looked like the Bounce Fashion Fund-raiser had exploded all over it. I tossed the sweater onto a pile near my closet, so that it could commune with the other Bounce clothes. *I'll sort them out later*, I told myself. "What is the Speed Spout Method, anyway?"

"Ugh! Arielle has decided that just answering the questions isn't challenging enough. So now, every time you mention a subject, she just blurts out *all* of the information she knows as fast as she can." Mitchie blew out a long sigh. "It's really annoying. I mean, she already talks at warp speed as it is. I know I was really excited about this Challenge when we first started — and I still am. But I have to say that part of me is looking forward to when it's over. All of these study sessions are making me a little crazy."

"Yeah . . ." Just then, my dog, Pizza, trotted into my room. She bounded onto the edge of my bed, then padded her way across my quilt to sit beside my hip. I petted her soft white fur and she licked the back of my hand, then settled down into a round dog doughnut. "Listen, about the study session yesterday . . . I just wanted you to know that Preston just sort of . . . crashed it."

There was a short pause on the other end of the line. "You mean you didn't invite Preston along on your *date*?" Mitchie teased.

I smiled. I should have known that Mitchie would understand. "Hardly."

"Why didn't you tell him to get lost?" Mitchie asked.

"Have you ever *tried* telling Preston to get lost?" I replied.

"Good point. But . . . how was it with Scott before Preston showed up? Any sparks?"

I could practically hear her eyebrows waggle as she said it. "Not exactly," I admitted, shuddering slightly. "Actually, I kind of managed to act like a complete idiot in front of Scott. Maybe it was lucky that Preston came along."

"I'm sure it wasn't that bad."

It was sweet of Mitchie to say so. . . . I hoped she was right.

"You know, Preston isn't so awful," Mitchie said. "I'm actually starting to like the guy. He's a lot smarter than he seems."

I didn't know what to say to that. In a way, I

knew what she meant. Preston had really impressed me at the study session the day before — he knew a lot about geography and current events. "Maybe . . ." I admitted. Then again, he'd also kept blowing straw wrappers at my head. "But he's still really annoying."

"Not half as annoying as Arielle," Mitchie shot back. She switched her voice to a high-pitched, nasal whine that actually sounded a lot like our teammate. "The average cockroach can live for several weeks without its head and roaches have been present on the planet for the past four million years and they are among some of the fastest-moving land insects and there's a roach living under my bed that I've nicknamed Earl and he really likes to eat brownie crumbs. . . ." She said all of this so fast that I barely understood a word of it. Still, it cracked me up.

"At least we have each other," I said, once I'd managed to control my giggles.

"Thank goodness," Mitchie said. "Okay, I'm about to steal another one of these muffins. I swear, I don't know how Akina makes them so good. I've used the same recipe, and it comes out tasting like soggy papier-mâché!"

"And I'm going to study," I said as I headed toward my desk with the cordless. Pizza gave me a reproachful look as I got up. "Apparently, there are a lot of facts I need to learn about cockroaches," I added, teasing.

"Have fun," Mitchie said, and we hung up.

I got my flash cards and brought them back to bed, where I set them out in piles according to subject — biology, physics, chemistry, space, and so on. Pizza sniffed gently at the earth science pile, then went back to sleep.

I picked up the biology cards. But as I flipped through the first few, a huge yawn practically took over my whole head. "I have to study a little longer," I told myself. "I can't go to sleep yet. Just a little longer . . ." But I couldn't stop the yawns from coming. My eyelids were drooping. . . . I could hardly keep them open.

"Which creature has the largest brain in relation to its body?" the flash card read.

Which creature? Which creature? Which — I was having trouble concentrating. The room was fuzzy. . . .

And the next thing I knew, my alarm clock was buzzing, announcing a brand-new day.

CHAPTER SIX

In: Me?!

"Hey, Amy!" The girl ran her fingers through her short blond hair as she walked past me in the hallway. She was wearing plaid-on-plaid, and I had no idea who she was.

"Hey . . . you," I replied. I was actually getting kind of good at pretending to know who people were.

Three blond sixthies smiled at me from beside their creamy yellow lockers. One of them — in leopard-print pants and a cheetah scarf — whispered to her friends as I walked by.

It was kind of creepy — and kind of cool at the same time.

At my old school, I'd practically been invisible. Not in a bad way — I had plenty of friends — but the place was too large to get to know everyone. I never expected everyone to wave and smile at me as I walked down the hall. We all just grabbed our books and headed to the next class.

But suddenly, I was capital-*F* Famous. In my own small world.

That morning, on the bus, I'd grabbed a pomegranate juice — a new addition to the free beverage menu, along with raspberry-kiwi — from the cooler at the front and headed to my seat. I'd flipped on the TV screen on the back of the seat behind mine and was absently watching the morning news as I twisted off the top. Naturally, I managed to spill juice on my jacket. And the minute I said, "Oh, shoot!" — almost before the syllables were out of my mouth — three girls and one boy were handing me tissues. Another girl ran to the front of the bus and grabbed a bottle of sparkling water, explaining that seltzer is great for removing stains. Then yet another girl took my jacket to the restroom at the rear of the bus and dried it under the hand dryer.

By the time we pulled up to the circular driveway in front of the huge Allington fountain, my jacket was as good as new. Maybe better, given that it was still slightly warm from the dryer.

And I didn't know *any* of those people.

No doubt about it, I said to myself as I waved to people in the halls, *this Fashion Fund-raiser has definitely raised my profile.*

"There you are?" Lucia said the minute I walked into English class. "We were just, like, waiting for you?"

She was sitting between Jenelle and Fiona, so I turned and looked behind me to see who she was talking to. But there wasn't anybody there.

Jenelle actually laughed as the truth dawned slowly. "You were waiting for *me*?" I repeated.

Fiona just rolled her eyes. That was more the kind of response I was used to.

But Lucia acted as if it was perfectly normal that the League — who never arrived for English class until twenty seconds before the chime — would be seated at their desks, watching the door for my entrance. "Um, yeah?" Lucia said, lifting her eyebrows in this "Of course, like, don't we always wait for you?" kind of way. She kicked a foot out from under her desk. "What do you think of these shoes?"

They were purple — half croc with suede at the toe — and had a dangerously high heel. They were the kind of shoes that looked like they'd be uncomfortable even when you were sitting down. Then again, they were pretty and looked great with Lucia's purple cashmere short-sleeved sweater. "They're . . . nice," I said finally.

Fiona let out a snort, and Lucia smiled smugly in her direction. "Fiona thinks that the toe is too, like, narrow?"

"*Rounded* is in," Fiona snapped. "Hel-*lo*?" She held out a foot bearing a moss-green wedge with a curvy heel. Sure enough, the toe was rounded.

"Oh." I slipped into the seat in front of Jenelle. "Well, I think you can do either. It's all about showing off your individual style."

Fiona glared laser beams at me. "Who says?"

Lucia dangled her foot in Fiona's direction. "Gianni Versace?"

Fiona huffed as Lucia dug around in her oversized purse, finally pulling out a copy of *Vogue*. Half of the pages were flagged with colored Post-it notes. "Okay, Amy, what do you think of the color orange?" she asked, carefully peeling open the magazine and tapping a glossy page with a pink fingernail.

The model was wearing a long orange wrap dress, orange scarf, orange hat, and had an orange handbag.

"Well, usually it's one of my favorite colors," I admitted. "But with that much, you kind of end up looking like a carrot."

"That's what I said," Jenelle agreed. "Except I said pumpkin, not carrot."

Lucia flashed a look at Fiona, who turned slightly pink. "Everyone's doing monochromatics," she said defensively. That was the moment that I noticed she was wearing a moss-green sheath dress that matched her shoes, tights, and bag. Oops.

"Not at this school?" Lucia shot back. "Here, it's all about, like, patterns?"

"Tell me about it," I agreed. Thanks to Bounce, plaid-on-plaid had practically taken over as the fashion statement of the moment.

"It's not going to last," Fiona muttered under her breath. I don't think anybody heard it but me.

Lucia planted her elbow on her desk and rested her chin in her palm. She gazed at me evenly with her dark chocolate eyes fringed with super-long lashes. "What do you think is the next big trend?"

I have to admit that it felt a little weird to have Lucia asking my opinion on clothes. Usually, she and Fiona thought that my outfits were raging rejects, at best. But all of a sudden, it was like I'd become some kind of fashion guru — at least, in Lucia's eyes. "Um . . ." I said at last, wracking my brain. I had no idea what the next trend was. Then again, I'd been looking over a bunch of stuff for the fund-raiser . . . *What have I seen?* Bounce had a huge selection of cool accessories. Suddenly, an image of a gorgeous grass-green handbag popped into my mind. It fastened with a buckle the size of my hand. "Bags with oversized hardware," I said at last.

"Like, big metal clasps and stuff?" Lucia asked.

"Definitely."

Lucia glanced at the tiny envelope wristlet on Fiona's desk, but she didn't mention it. Instead, she said just about the last thing I expected her to say. "So, Amy — do you want to go to the Blakesley Jones concert Friday night?"

For a minute, I thought that maybe she was just asking me in a general way. You know, in the way you might say, "Do you want to go to an Astros game? Oh, well, me too. Too bad we can't afford it." But then she added, "I've got an extra ticket. They're box seats, so we'll have a great view."

Fiona's eyes had narrowed so much that I wondered if she could see anything but eyelashes. *She doesn't want me to come*, I thought. I felt the words "No, thanks," rising in my throat. . . .

"It's going to be awesome," Jenelle said warmly, leaning forward in her desk slightly. "I love Blakesley Jones."

"Who doesn't?" Lucia gave a dreamy sigh. "He's *so* good?" She batted her lashes, completely oblivious to Fiona's rage.

I felt a slow smile seep across my face. *Fiona doesn't want me there — and the rest of the League does. And how often do you get a chance to make Fiona mad* and *go to a Blakesley Jones concert at the same time?* I knew I'd probably have to beg my parents for about three hours in order to get them to agree. Then again, we'd be in a private box. And it wasn't on a school night. *If I promise to be home by nine thirty*, I thought, *I might just have a shot.* "Lucia," I said, "I'd love to go."

This was an opportunity not to be missed.

"Hey!" I said happily as I yanked open the front door. "What's up?"

Mitchie was standing there, holding a pair of Rollerblades. "Tell me that you want to go do something fun," she said. "If I study anymore, my head will explode."

"I want to go do something fun," I told her. "And I don't want your head to blow up."

"Then I've come to the right place," she said happily. "I was thinking we could blade over to the park."

"Sounds perfect." I'd been sitting at my desk all afternoon — studying, of course — and an hour moving around outside was just what I needed. "I just need to get my skates. Come on in," I told her, holding the door wider so that she could step inside.

Mitchie placed her Rollerblades neatly by the front door and followed me into the living room. "Cool house. What's that?"

This is what everyone asks when they walk into my living room. That's because there's a giant sculpture made of black wire that divides the living area from the dining area. It's a series of gears and levers, and it reaches all the way to the ceiling. At the top are two brass globes. "It's a Dondelo," I told her.

"Oh." Mitchie nodded seriously as if that explained everything, which made me laugh.

"Watch." I flipped a switch on the wall, and the Dondelo started to hum. The gears spun, the levers levered. Finally, one of the balls at the top shifted from the right to the left, and the Dondelo began to rock back and forth.

"Crazy!" Mitchie's eyes were wide.

"It's art," I explained as I shut off the switch. The humming stopped and the rocking slowed as the Dondelo's gears wound down. "One of my dad's students made it as a gift. It's named after him — Jim Dondelo."

"For the man who has everything," Mitchie said dryly.

"Right." I laughed. "My mom was like, 'What's so wrong with a gift certificate?' But now she thinks it's kind of cool."

"It's *totally* cool! But my mom would *freak* if my dad brought that home," Mitchie said as she followed me down the hall. "I mean, if I buy a new shirt, she makes me throw an old one out. I have no idea what she'd do if I came home with a prehistoric wire robot thingie."

I giggled as I dug around in the bottom of my closet and finally came up with my blades. "Okay! Ready!" When I turned around, I saw that Mitchie was studying the mountain of clothes parked near my bureau.

Our eyes caught for a moment before she asked, "Fashion Fund-raiser stuff?"

"Yeah," I admitted.

She nodded and didn't say anything else as we made our way down the hall. A sudden chilly feeling of unease had just come over me, although I wasn't sure why. I mean, I knew that Mitchie wasn't wild about the League (okay, Understatement Alert — she couldn't stand them) and I knew that she wasn't into fashion. But that didn't mean she cared if *I* helped out, right? And I'd been studying like crazy for the Challenge lately, so it wasn't like I was doing one thing and not the other. . . .

A cool breeze hit my face as we opened the front door and stepped outside. It was late November and starting to feel kind of fall-like. Our lawn was covered with crunchy leaves. The trees don't really change color here the way they do in other parts of the country. I went to visit my aunt in Massachusetts one October, and I couldn't believe all of the different shades of red and yellow and orange. (I couldn't believe how cold it was, either.) Here, the leaves just kind of turn brown and fall off the trees. You can still rake them into piles and jump in them, though.

My brother was in the driveway, riding up the cement on his skateboard. As he neared the garage, he crouched a little, as if he was going to pull a trick.

"Hey, Kirk!" Mitchie called as the board flipped into the air. Kirk fell on his butt as it rolled away, coming to a stop on the grass. This is his new hobby: falling off his skateboard.

"Ouch." Kirk groaned and sat in the driveway a moment, glaring at the skateboard as if it had stabbed him in the back.

Laughing, Mitchie reached down and grabbed it. "Nice deck," she said casually.

"There's something wrong with it," Kirk grumbled. "I think it's unbalanced."

"Why? Because you can't stay on it?" I teased.

Kirk ignored me as Mitchie flipped over the board and inspected the wheels. "Your trucks look okay," she said. "Let me try it." She dropped her blades on the grass and stepped lightly onto the board, gliding down the driveway in an elegant *S*. Just before she reached the sidewalk, she pushed down hard with her right foot. She rose into the air as the board flipped under her feet. She landed perfectly as the skateboard's wheels met the pavement and kept on rolling.

"Whoa," Kirk breathed when Mitchie came to a stop. She gave the board a kick and it flipped obediently into her hand.

"I think it's okay," she said, walking back to join us. She handed the board to Kirk, who was still sitting on his rear end in the middle of our driveway.

"Where did you learn to do a pop shove-it?" he asked as he hauled himself to his feet.

Mitchie shrugged, but she looked flattered. "Just messing around on my board. There's a skate park near my house. You should try it out sometime."

"That would be awesome!" Kirk said, just as I said, "He'll probably break his neck."

Kirk shot me a sideways glare. "Why do you have so many cool friends?" he demanded. "It just doesn't make sense. Listen," he added, turning to Mitchie, "if I come to the park sometime, would you show me a few tricks?"

Suddenly, Mitchie looked a little shy. "Sure," she said.

"Great!" Kirk beamed.

They stood there for a moment, smiling at each other.

"Oookay . . . we're headed to the park," I said finally. I grabbed Mitchie's in-line skates and handed them to her. "See you later, Tony Hawk."

"Ha-ha. You're so hilarious." Kirk flapped a hand in my direction, as if he was waving off a fly.

I laughed, and Mitchie and I started down the street.

"Your brother's funny," Mitchie said after a moment.

"Yeah," I admitted. Kirk and I give each other a hard time, but basically he's okay. When he's not being annoying.

Mitchie bent down and picked up a twig. "So . . ." she said casually as she tapped the twig against a tree trunk. "Who else does he think is cool?"

"What?"

"Kirk said that you have cool friends," Mitchie explained. "I was just wondering who else he's met."

"Oh, well, he knows my friend Elise," I said. She was from my old school, and we'd been buds for years. Then again, Kirk had never really thought Elise was cool — he always said that she talks too much. So who else could he have been talking about? "And I guess he knows Jenelle," I remembered.

"Oh." Mitchie tossed aside the stick and made a sour face, like she'd just accidentally sipped some ancient milk.

I was going to let it go . . . but then . . . I don't know, I just couldn't. I mean, Jenelle has always been nice to me. She's my friend. And it's weird to have two good friends who can't stand each other. "What do you have against her?" I asked.

With a sigh, Mitchie stopped walking and turned to face me. "Remember how I told you that Fiona cut off my hair?" Her voice was quiet and she was very still.

"When you were sleeping." I nodded, remembering the story. It had sent a chill through me when I heard it. "You were at her house for a sleepover."

"Well . . ." Mitchie turned away, and I studied the sharp lines of her profile — her angular jaw, her pointed nose. With her creamy complexion, she looked like a statue carved from a piece of marble. "Jenelle was there, too," Mitchie said at last. "She could have stopped Fiona, and she didn't. That's all." She looked back at me, and her dark eyes landed on mine like a weight. She didn't look sad, exactly, or mad, exactly, but more . . . disappointed. And I realized at that moment that Jenelle must have been her good friend before that happened.

"I had no idea," I said. I didn't know what else to say.

"Now you know." Mitchie pressed her lips together in a stubborn line. After a moment, she turned and started walking again. I fell into step beside her, and neither one of us spoke.

Yeah, now I knew. And part of me wished that I didn't.

"Protons," I muttered to myself as I flipped over a flash card and glanced at the question on the next one. "Manatees," I said, without even checking the answer. I didn't need to — I'd studied these cards so hard that they were practically stamped into my brain. Next card: "Photosynthesis." Finally, I was getting into a rhythm for the Challenge.

"Hey, I hear you're going to the concert tonight," Anderson said as he perched on the lab stool beside me.

"No time to talk," I told him, flipping to another card. "Need to study." We still had five minutes before the start of science class, and I wanted to ram as many facts into my skull as possible before the bell.

"Do we have a quiz today?" he asked, concern clouding his clear blue eyes. He clawed open his messenger bag and yanked out the text.

"It's okay." I put my hand over his to stop him from flipping through the book like a maniac. "I've got the first round of the Academic Challenge on Saturday," I explained.

Anderson looked at me for a long time, studying my face. "You look kind of tired," he said after a moment.

"I am tired," I admitted. "I got up early to look over the sample questions. And I got to bed a little late."

Anderson smiled.

"What?" I asked.

"You're a mystery, Amy Flowers."

"I am?" I tend to think of myself as just about the least mysterious person in the world. Kirk always says that I'm an open book — one in large type. You can read my face from a mile away. "What do you mean?"

"I mean, why would anyone volunteer to take an extra test?" he asked.

"It's not a test."

Anderson cocked an eyebrow. "Do they ask you hard questions?"

"Well . . . yes."

His blue eyes were steady. "And if you get them wrong, you fail, right? You lose the Challenge?"

"That's true, but —"

"And you've been studying for it, haven't you?" Anderson pointed out. I didn't even need to reply because Anderson was eyeing the flash cards right in front of me. "Sounds like a test to me."

I had to admit it — he had a point. "But it doesn't count for anything," I said. "It's more like a game."

He patted my shoulder gently. "Well, I hope you win," he said.

"Yeah." An image of Mitchie's face flashed in my brain. I knew how much this Challenge meant to her. "I hope so, too."

"Hi, guys," Jenelle said. She leaned against our lab table and smiled at me. But the smile she gave Anderson was a lot brighter — by several kilowatts.

"Hey, Jenelle." Anderson's round face was beaming.

All of this smiley-ness made me smile, too. I just couldn't help it.

Then Fiona walked up and joined us. *Way to make my smiley-ness disappear.* She looked from Jenelle to Anderson and huffed out a little sigh.

"So, Amy, are you ready for the fund-raiser this weekend?" Jenelle asked me.

"Yeah . . . but I've got the first round of the Challenge that afternoon," I told her. "I may have to be a few minutes late." I pulled a purple notebook out of my bag and flipped it open. "Here's all of my notes — it's got everything in it, like what outfits go together and which models should wear what."

"No problem," Jenelle said. "You've got everything so organized, the rest of us can set things up."

Fiona craned her neck to look at my notes. I expected her to make some kind of mean comment, but all she said was, "This should make things easy." Then she held out her hand.

I hesitated, reluctant to hand my notebook to Fiona. Part of me didn't trust her with it. *Don't be crazy,* said another part. *She wants this fund-raiser to be a success as much as you do.* Not that I had much of a choice, anyway. I was going to be at the Challenge, and someone had to set up. "I'll try to be on time," I said quickly as I handed over the notebook.

"Just be on time to walk down the runway," Jenelle replied with a smile.

"We'll handle everything else," Fiona said. She was looking at the notebook, not at me, when she said it, and I was surprised at the sincerity in her voice. "I brought the music for the show, and I e-mailed the brochure so Lucia could get it printed.

She showed me a copy this morning — it looks pretty good. I just hope we can pull this off." For once, she didn't sound mean or catty — just like she wanted the fund-raiser to be a success. Normally, I probably would have soaked up some of Fiona's stress. I'm spongy that way. But in this situation it actually made me feel a little better. *She wouldn't ruin the fund-raiser*, I thought. *After all, that would just make her look bad.*

"It's going to be great," I told her.

"Everyone's going," Anderson put in. "Even the guys."

Fiona blinked at him, almost as if she was really seeing him for the first time. "Really?" she asked.

Anderson nodded. "Everyone."

Fiona smiled at him. It was a nice smile — like she was grateful for what he'd said.

Too bad she doesn't smile more often, I thought. *It almost makes her look like someone you'd want to be friends with.*

CHAPTER SEVEN

In: Bright saris
Out: I'm sorry's

"Try one of these," Jenelle said, passing me a small, flaky pastry. The flakes melted on my tongue, dissolving to reveal something tangy inside.

"What is it?" I asked.

"Lucia's parents' specialty," Jenelle replied. "Chile relleno pie. So good." With a smile, she popped one into her mouth.

"Isn't this, like, the best concert ever?" Lucia asked as she peered through the glass. We were in a skybox and had an incredible view of the stage, where Blakesley Jones had just appeared in a burst of pyrotechnics. His backup dancers were

120

dressed in bright, colorful Indian saris, and they danced between tall jets of sparks as he sang his huge hit, "Hot Curry."

"It's definitely the best concert I've ever been to," I admitted as I looked around the skybox. We had the place to ourselves, and there was a table loaded with delicious things to eat and sodas. It really was an amazing concert so far. Of course, I didn't have all that much to compare it to, given that the last concert I'd attended had been chamber music at my dad's university. And before that, Kirk's band in our garage. If you want to call that music.

"It's okay," Fiona said from her place on the leather couch. She yawned slightly, then took a sip of her diet cola. "It would have been better if we were in the front row."

Lucia wrinkled her nose. "Oh, ugh, there's always some gross sweaty guy in the front row?" she replied. "Or some crazy lady throwing stuff on the stage?"

"This is better," Jenelle agreed. She smiled at me, and I tried my best to smile back. But I'd been feeling weird around Jenelle ever since my conversation with Mitchie. Like I didn't know her as well as I'd thought.

"Whatever," Fiona said. She crossed her legs

and leaned back on the couch, not even looking out at the show.

"I love those outfits?" Lucia said as the dancers held long, sheer scarves over their heads, letting them flutter on the breeze created by a giant wind machine.

"The colors are so brilliant," I agreed. They made me think of flower petals or magic carpets.

"I read that color is going to be really in this spring?" Lucia said, casting me a sideways glance. "Like, nobody's going to be wearing black anymore?"

"People will always wear black," Fiona snapped. "It goes with everything and it's slimming." I found this statement kind of funny — especially since she was wearing a blue skirt and a red top. Not a stitch of black in sight.

"What do *you* think, Amy?" Lucia asked.

I couldn't resist a dig at Fiona. "I think people are sick of black," I said.

"Me too." Lucia's words were soft — I barely heard her — and she touched the glass delicately with her finger, as if she wanted to reach out to those beautiful scarves.

Fiona — who apparently has some kind of super-human hearing — grunted.

Ha-ha, I thought at her. *Looks like you're not the "expert" anymore.*

"What do you think about open-toed shoes?" Lucia asked suddenly, turning to face me.

"Um . . . I think they look cute. But I never know if you can wear tights with them or not."

"You can't," Fiona snapped. As if anyone had asked her.

"Do you have any predictions for next season?" Lucia pulled her long, shiny brown hair over one shoulder. "I mean, beyond what the magazines are saying."

Predictions? That was hard to say. Honestly, I'd never really planned my outfits based on what was in fashion. I just wore what I liked, which sometimes meant some weird stuff — vintage, or things I'd sewn myself. I was tempted to say something peculiar — like green visors — just to see if Lucia would show up in one the next day. *Actually, that gives me an idea. . . .* "I think charity work will be in," I said.

"Charity work?" Lucia looked stunned. She turned to Jenelle.

"All the stars are doing it," Jenelle pointed out. "And regular people, too, like at Amy's mom's Save the Earth gala."

"You won't be anyone unless you're doing good deeds," I said. "Charity is the new accessory."

"That's stupid," Fiona volunteered from her place on the couch.

But Lucia's eyes had glazed over, as if she was trying to envision herself in a future that was still a little murky. "What kind of charity?"

"Oh, any kind. In fact, I was thinking we could do something more with the Fashion Fund-raiser," I explained as a new idea took shape in my mind. "We could donate a portion of our profits to the Book Fund. They give out free books to under-privileged kids."

"That money is supposed to go to the library," Fiona pointed out. "The *Allington* library."

"We don't have to give away all of the money," I said. "Just some of it. It's for a good cause."

"It's perfect?" Lucia gushed. "It's, like, the perfect combo of fashion and, like, goodness?"

"Sounds great," Jenelle agreed.

Fiona looked at Jenelle. Then she looked at Lucia. Her blue eyes flashed dangerously. But she didn't protest. "Fine," she said at last. "Do whatever you want."

It was a teeny-tiny moment of triumph, and I felt like throwing a teeny-tiny parade.

Just then, there was a knock on the door, and before anyone could say "come in," Preston burst into the room, followed by Anderson.

"Hey!" Preston said as he made his way over to the snack table. "I heard you guys were up here."

For a split second, I wondered how he found us. Then I wondered *why* he found us. But when I noticed the shy smile that Jenelle was giving Anderson, I realized the whole situation: *She must have told Anderson to meet her here.*

"Hey, Preston," Fiona said, looking at him from beneath her thick black eyelashes.

"Hi. Oh, man! How come your snacks are so much better than ours?" Preston asked as he started filling up a plate at the table.

"Because we had them catered?" Lucia said.

"Lucia's family," Jenelle explained to Anderson. Lucia's family owned seventeen restaurants in Houston.

"I thought this was a restricted area," Fiona said slowly, giving Anderson the eye.

"We're in the box three doors down," Preston explained. "Nice outfit, by the way." Fiona beamed for a moment, until Preston added, "You look like last week's picture of Amy in the *Allington Observer.*"

I choked on my mini-burrito. Fiona was wearing a blue plaid skirt and a red plaid top. I hadn't wanted to mention it, but she really did look like that photo.

Fiona's cheeks turned red. "I do not," she said, but she sounded uncertain.

Strangely, I felt a quick flash of sympathy for Fiona. I mean, she was used to being Queen Bug, Head Fashionista, the Person with Miles of Style. The rest of the League used to take their cues from her . . . and now, even though I was glad that Lucia didn't feel the need to dress exactly according to Fiona's rules, I felt a little bad for Fiona.

"The only reason I'm wearing this stupid outfit is to help promote the Fashion Fund-raiser," Fiona went on. "Otherwise, I wouldn't be caught dead in this stupid Eclectic Dork look."

And my sympathetic feelings flew out the window.

Preston just shrugged. "Hey, Amy. What are you doing here? Aren't you supposed to be studying?"

"Aren't you?" I shot back.

He flashed me a cocky grin. "Nah," he said confidently. "I'm not the one who's going to freeze up on national TV."

126

"I'm *not* going to freeze," I said. But immediately, an image of myself with a deer-in-the-headlights look on my face flashed into my brain. *Great.*

Preston laughed. "We'll see. Maybe we won't even get to the final round, anyway." He plopped down on the couch and Fiona got up.

She crossed the room and planted herself between Anderson and Jenelle. "Oh, look," she said, peering down to where Blakesley Jones had just hopped onto an enormous merry-go-round. "He's doing 'Carnival Ride.' Isn't that your favorite song, Jenelle?" She turned so that her back was completely to Anderson.

For a split second, my eyes and Preston's clicked. Then he bit into his enchilada and looked away. But I had the weird feeling that he was feeling the same way I was — annoyed at Fiona. She didn't think Anderson and Jenelle made a good couple, just because Jenelle was two inches taller than Anderson.

So stupid.

It was hard to believe that Fiona actually cared about that.

The only thing that was harder to believe was that it looked like her attitude actually bothered

Preston as much as it bothered me. But I guess it made sense. Anderson was his friend, after all.

It was one thing we could agree on.

"How did it go?" Mr. Pearl asked the minute he saw me. "How did you feel about the test, Ms. Flowers? Was it too easy for you? Hm? Did you have to ask for harder questions?" He took a sip from his giant-sized commuter mug of coffee and widened his eyes at me. The team was gathered in the corner of the cafeteria-slash-auditorium at Episcopal Day School. We were surrounded by students from other schools — there must have been at least fifty teams. Normally, an auditorium packed with middle school students would have been deafening. But this crowd was pretty subdued. I think everyone was feeling nervous.

We'd just finished taking our paper tests, and everyone looked a little stressed out, except for Preston, who was munching happily on a powdered sugar doughnut. I guessed he'd been raiding the snack tables at the edge of the cafetorium.

"It was harder than I thought," I admitted.

"Like what?" Arielle asked. "Give me a sample question."

"Well, there were a couple of weird biology

questions, like 'What's the only animal that never sleeps?'"

"Bullfrog," Arielle and Scott said at the same time.

Terrific. Way to look like a genius.

"Is that what you put down?" Mitchie asked. Her face was really tense.

I hesitated, not wanting to admit that I'd screwed up. But I couldn't lie, either. "Um, no," I admitted. "I said shark."

"They sleep," Arielle said.

"With their eyes open," Scott added. "All fish do."

"Well, one question won't sink us!" Mr. Pearl said cheerfully. "No worries, no worries! This is our year, I'm telling you!"

"Were there any other tough questions?" Arielle asked. She looked like she was about to pounce on me or something.

"I think the rest were okay," I said. This was only a small, tiny, slight exaggeration. Actually, there were a few questions that I'd been unsure about. But I didn't want to look like an idiot in front of Scott any more than I already had. "How did everyone else do?"

"Pretty good, I think," Scott said. "There were one or two really tough geometry questions."

"The literature part was pretty easy," Mitchie said. "But the history section was brutal. How did you do, Preston?"

Preston had to finish chewing his doughnut before he could answer. There was a slight dusting of powdered sugar on the lapel of his navy jacket. Allington insists on jackets for boys and skirts for girls whenever we're representing the school at an official function. Technically, Preston had conformed to the dress code . . . although his hair was stylishly messy and he was wearing untied sneakers with his dress slacks. *He sure looks confident*, I thought. *I'm surprised Mitchie even bothered asking him how it went.* "Cake," Preston said at last.

"That easy?" Mitchie asked.

"No, they just brought out some cake," he said, craning his neck to look toward the rear of the cafetorium. "Ooh, chocolate. Anyone else want a slice?"

Everyone shook their head except for Mr. Pearl, who handed his mug over to Preston. "Would you mind refilling this? There's a big urn at the end of the table. And just a bit of sugar. A bit, bit, bit. Tiny amount. I'm watching my waistline, ho-ho!" He patted his round belly.

"We're toast, aren't we?" Mitchie asked as she watched Preston hurry off. She was nibbling on a thumbnail.

"We're fine, we're fine!" Mr. Pearl said heartily. "This is a great team! Oh, look, I think they're about ready to announce the scores."

Sure enough, a tall woman in a red business suit had just walked up to the podium. "Good afternoon, everyone," she said. "My name is Pamela Dredge, and I'm assistant to the headmaster here at Episcopal Day. Thank you for coming to the first round of the annual Academic Challenge."

She went through a long boring explanation of how the scoring worked. Basically, the deal was that it would have taken way too much time for every team to face off, so Round One consisted of paper tests. Each team member took a test in his or her special area. The two teams with the combined highest scores would be the ones to face off in the final.

I took a deep breath in through my nose and out through my mouth. According to my dad, this is supposed to help relax you, but I didn't feel relaxed. I felt like I was about to faint.

"The top team from this year's first round

is . . ." I felt my heart hammering in my chest as Ms. Dredge looked down at her notes. "Karter."

A cheer went up from the far corner of the room as the Karter team burst into whoops. The rest of the room clapped politely.

"I knew it," Mitchie muttered.

"And, in second place, we have the team from St. Joseph's," Ms. Dredge said. Four kids in the front row stood up, pumping their fists in the air.

So obnoxious, I thought, glaring at them. *Stupid St. Joseph's.*

All of the air blew out of Mitchie and she seemed to crumple a little as we stood there. That was it, then. We'd blown it.

"Wait, wait," Ms. Dredge said into the microphone. She motioned for the St. Joseph's team to take their seats. "I'm not finished. In second place, we have the team from St. Joseph's *and* the team from Allington Academy. For the first time ever, we have a tie." Our team burst into a cheer, pumping our fists in the air. I let out a crazy scream and wrapped Mitchie in a hug. We weren't out! We were in!

"Hush, hush, people!" Mr. Pearl said, gesturing for us to sit down. "She's giving instructions."

"This means that we're going to a sudden-death

elimination round," Ms. Dredge explained from her place behind the podium. "The winner will face off against Karter in the final round next week. Will the teams from St. Joseph's and Allington Academy please take the stage?"

Two men started to unfold chairs on the stage, four on the left, four on the right. Mitchie and Scott headed up the aisle, but I hesitated just a moment. The Fashion Fund-raiser was supposed to start in about forty-five minutes. *Do I have time for this sudden-death round?* I asked myself. *Arielle could take my place. . . .*

Mitchie suddenly turned and looked at me, eyebrows raised. "Coming?" she mouthed. She motioned for me to join her.

Just then, Preston appeared at my elbow. "What did I miss?" he asked, handing the commuter mug to Mr. Pearl.

"Sudden death," I told him. "We've got to face off against St. Joseph's."

He looked sadly at his slice of cake.

"Later," I told him, placing the plate on the table in front of Mr. Pearl. I gritted my teeth and headed up the aisle. The Fashion Fund-raiser would have to wait, too. It was go time.

"Good luck!" our teacher told us. "Knock them dead! You can do it! This is your time to shine!"

He took a swig of coffee and grimaced. "Oh, ugh, Preston! I said a *little* sugar, not no sugar at all!"

"Don't screw up!" Arielle called as we made our way to the stage.

We climbed the steps to the stage and I took my seat beside Mitchie. The St. Joseph's team was right across from us, at a slight angle so that the audience could see their faces. A girl wearing her hair in a tight French braid gave me a little smile — it was a smile that said, "We're going to crush you." The guy beside her — round face, even rounder glasses — seemed to be trying to stare Scott down. Scott looked uncomfortable, and I didn't blame him. This team was *intense*.

"All right." Ms. Dredge stood before us, microphone in hand. She was short and solidly built, and looked like a fire hydrant in her red suit. "The way this works is this: I will ask each team a question. Correct answers are worth one point. At the end of each round, if the scores are equal, we will move on to the next question. If the scores are unequal, the team with the higher score will be the winner."

Okay, so if we both get the first question right, we move on, I thought. *And if we both get the first question wrong, we move on. But if one of us gets it wrong and the other gets it right — game over.*

"First question," she said, and a hush fell over the room. "For St. Joseph's. What is the driest location on the planet?"

"Antarctica," French Braid Girl said.

"That is correct."

French Braid smiled smugly at me. *Loser*, she mouthed.

The next question was ours. "What was the working title for *Gone with the Wind*, by Margaret Mitchell?"

I looked over at Mitchie, but she had it covered. "Before publication, the book was known as 'Ba! Ba! Black Sheep.'"

"Correct."

The auditorium burst into applause as the assistant to the headmaster announced that we would go on to the next round.

Whew. Part of me couldn't believe that Mitchie actually knew the answer to that. And another part of me couldn't believe that *Gone with the Wind* had started out with such a lame title. And yet *another* part of me didn't care about any of it — we were still in the competition.

Question after question. I answered something about the sun correctly and nearly fainted in my chair, I was so relieved. But St. Joseph's wasn't getting anything wrong!

We could be here forever, I thought as I looked up at the clock on the far wall. Half an hour had passed by already. I felt a trickle of sweat tickle its way down my spine. The fund-raiser was going to start without me.

"The next question is a math question," Ms. Dredge announced. "X is a two-digit number. Add the digits, then subtract the sum from the original number. Then add the digits of the result. Is the answer a) eleven, b) forty-four, c) nine, or d) not enough information?"

The kid with the round face snapped to attention. "D) not enough information," he said.

Scott looked over at me, and I could read on his face that he'd known the answer — and that the round-faced kid had gotten it wrong.

"That is not correct. The answer to that question is nine. It's always nine."

The auditorium let out a gasp as the woman turned to our team. Round-Face Boy looked like he was about to pass out or barf on his shoes or something.

My heart was pounding in my ears. An opening. We finally had an opening!

"Which stars have the lowest temperatures — a) blue, b) yellow-white, or c) red?"

I felt my stomach sink. *I know this*, I thought. *I*

know it. It's just at the tip of my brain. . . . Seconds ticked by on the clock on the wall across from me. *We could win we could win wecouldwinwecouldwin,* my brain repeated unhelpfully. I heard Arielle's words: "Don't screw up!" *I should know the answer to this,* I thought. *I studied it.*

But it wasn't coming to me.

"B) yellow-white?" I asked.

The woman held me in a steady gaze. "I'm sorry," she said at last. "That is incorrect. The answer is a) blue."

I felt my face burn as the crowd let out a groan. I glanced over at Mitchie, but she wasn't even looking in my direction. Her jaw was set, and her face looked hard.

I'd let everyone down. I'd single-handedly blown our chance at winning. . . .

Now I felt like *I* might barf on my shoes.

"All right. Another question for St. Joseph's," Ms. Dredge announced. "More than half of the coastline of the United States is located in what state?"

The St. Joseph's team looked at each other. French Braid whispered something to Round Face, who nodded. The guy next to him nodded as well. "California," he said.

"That is not correct," Ms. Dredge said.

My head nearly rolled off my neck. *Another chance! Oh, please, ask a science question,* I thought. *Let me redeem myself. Or ask a literature question and let Mitchie win this thing so I can get to the Fashion Fund-raiser. . . .*

"The answer is Alaska." Ms. Dredge looked primly over the tops of her reading glasses. "And now a question for Allington Academy. What is the only city in the world located on two continents?"

I nearly stifled a groan. *Geography!* Scott looked over at Preston — that was his specialty. Supposedly.

But Preston didn't smile and he didn't flash his usual cocky look. *Omigosh,* I thought desperately. *He doesn't know the answer! We're doomed. Dooooooooooomed! I'm going to be stuck in this Academic Challenge for the rest of my life. . . .*

"Istanbul, Turkey," Preston said.

For a moment, the auditorium was perfectly quiet. I could hear the blood rushing in my ears.

"That is correct," said Ms. Dredge, and in the next moment we were cheering so loudly that I couldn't even hear her announcing that we had won, and were going on to the finals. And all because of Preston!

Mr. Pearl and Arielle rushed the stage to join us. "Wonderful, wonderful! That was spectacular!" Mr. Pearl gushed. "You had me worried for a moment there — ha-ha! Just for a minute, mind you, a split second, but I knew you'd come out on top!"

"What happened to my cake?" Preston asked, eyeing the empty plate in Mr. Pearl's hand.

Our teacher looked down at the plate with huge eyes. "I ate it!" he said, sounding completely surprised.

"I can't believe you missed that question about stars," Arielle said to me.

I was very proud of myself for not strangling her.

"Everyone misses a question now and again," Mr. Pearl said. "Nobody's perfect! Nobody's perfect!"

"But we have to be perfect if we want to beat Karter," Mitchie said. Her mouth was twisted into a tense line. "I mean, the finals are on Tuesday afternoon! We're going to need to study our brains out."

"Not our brains," Scott teased. "We need them."

"Hey, let's head over to Daily Blend now," Preston suggested. "We can celebrate *and* study!"

"A fine idea!" Mr. Pearl gushed. "Brilliant!"

Mitchie looked at me expectantly.

I winced. "I can't go," I told her. "The Fashion Fund-raiser is this afternoon. I'm already late." The part I didn't say was: *Your mom is supposed to give me a ride back to the school, remember?*

For a long moment, nobody spoke.

"Oh," Mitchie said at last. "Right." But she was giving me a Look. I wasn't exactly sure what it meant — something like, "Are you seriously ditching us for the fashion thingie?"

"I'm sorry," I told her.

Mitchie nodded. "Okay."

But her face didn't look like it was okay. I knew I'd let her down. And I was letting her down again.

I'll make it up to her with Karter, I promised myself. *I'll study every minute of every day until the finals. I swear.*

The minute the Fashion Fund-raiser is over.

CHAPTER EIGHT

Out: Me.

When we reached the Allington auditorium, the doors were already closed. I could hear people cheering and the music Fiona had selected pumping through the walls. My heart was racing, but I was glad that it sounded as if there were plenty of people there.

"We can't get in this way," Mitchie pointed out.

I knew what she meant — we could get in, of course, but there was no way to get backstage now that the show had started. "Back door," I told her and we raced through the school exit and around to the rear of the building. I yanked open

141

the door and stepped into the darkness of backstage — and was almost knocked over by a girl in purple plaid.

"Sorry!" she whispered, and a moment later my eyes adjusted to the light and I recognized Brooke Rosen. Her hair was crimped and wild around her face, and she had on extreme eye shadow that looked amazing with the purple outfit. "Hey!" She grinned. Then she rushed toward the stage.

A moment later someone walked off the stage, nearly running into me from the other direction. "Um, excuse me?" I could tell just from the non-question question that it was Lucia. "Amy? So you finally made it?" She didn't wait for an answer but headed toward the dressing room at the back.

At the sound of my name, someone turned around. It was Jenelle. She had been standing in a wing holding a clipboard, but when she saw me, she hurried over. "I'm so glad you're here!" she said as the crowd let out a cheer.

"What's that?" I asked, trying to peer over her shoulder.

"The crowd has been going *nuts* every time Brooke walks out on stage," Jenelle explained. "They love her."

"I knew it!"

"And the outfits are a huge hit," Jenelle went on.

"Are you serious?" Mitchie asked. She was standing by a rack of clothes, holding up the black sleeve of a sweater with a cheetah collar. "Who wears this crazy stuff?"

"Everyone at our school, apparently," Jenelle replied.

Mitchie gave a "Whatever" shrug and the two of them just stood there for a moment. As if they were each waiting for the other to speak or make a move.

It was a little creepy, to tell you the truth.

"So, uh . . . do I need to get changed?" I asked.

"Actually, Fiona asked Voe to take your place on the runway." Jenelle tapped her clipboard. "We held the show for ten minutes, but then we really had to get started. . . ."

"Oh." It was hard to keep the disappointment out of my voice.

Jenelle looked apologetic. "I could pull her out. . . ."

"No, no," I said quickly. "It's okay." I mean, I was disappointed. But I understood. *The show must go on, right?*

From the stage, I heard Fiona's voice calling the show. "This lovely little number is a Classique

143

original, featuring rickrack at the hem and decorative stitching." She had the right voice for the job — low and snobby enough to make what she was saying sound important.

"Listen, I'd better take off," Mitchie said suddenly.

"You're not staying?" Jenelle asked. I was actually surprised by how disappointed she sounded.

Mitchie looked surprised, too. But she gave her head a slight shake. "Not my thing." Then she gave me one last look. "See you later."

"Maybe we can get together to study tomorrow?" I asked.

"Yeah," Mitchie said. "Maybe." There was a slight flash of dim light from the parking lot as she opened the door. She was just a black shadow against the gray. Then the door swung slowly shut behind her, and I was back in the darkness.

Jenelle touched my arm gently. "Everything okay?"

"Oh, I just . . ." I sighed. "I think Mitchie's mad because I nearly blew the Challenge for us today."

Jenelle pressed her lips together in a grim line. "She'll get over it," she said after a moment.

"I don't know — the Challenge is really important to her. And I kind of let her down."

Jenelle looked back at the door, as if she could see Mitchie through it. "I know how you feel," she said quietly. Two models rushed past us in silence, but Jenelle didn't move. She didn't even seem to notice they were there. "You can't make someone forgive you," she said. "They either will, or they won't. In your case, I'll bet she will. Mitchie's handled worse."

I thought about what Mitchie said about Jenelle — how she hadn't stopped Fiona from cutting off her hair. I was positive that was what Jenelle was talking about. I wanted to ask her about it — to hear her side of the story — but I didn't dare. It didn't seem like it was my business.

"Want to watch the show?" Jenelle asked suddenly. "There's a great view from the wings. Wait, hold on," she said as Pear — who looked amazing with crimped hair and a leopard-print dress — started to brush past us. "Hem isn't straight." She gave Pear's skirt a delicate yank, and it settled back into place. Then she stepped back to let Pear pass.

"Accessories are by De Rigeur," Fiona announced as Pear took the stage. "They feature fine leather and solid brass fittings."

Pear paused so that the audience could admire her deep-red handbag. They clapped politely, but nothing like the way they had cheered when Brooke walked out.

"I really do love that bag," I told Jenelle. "The clasp is so cool." It was an elaborate buckle covered in etched flowers. Pear was wearing a matching pair of shoes with buckles on the front.

"It's funny how trends come and go," Jenelle said. "Buckles on shoes — that started in the middle of the seventeenth century, and it just keeps coming back."

I'd never really thought about it that way before, but Jenelle had a point. "Pear's look — inspired by Pilgrims," I said, imitating Fiona's haughty tone.

Jenelle gave a little giggle-snort. "We should have given her a tall hat with a buckle," she joked.

"That really would have completed the look," I said, and we both laughed.

Two more models took the stage, and I glanced out into the audience. The auditorium was packed — it looked like half of the school had turned out to watch the show. "There's Anderson," I said, noticing him in the fifth row with a couple of his friends. Surprisingly, Preston was sitting two seats from him at the end of the row. *When did he sneak in?* I wondered.

"Yeah . . ." Jenelle said. I noticed the muscles in her jaw working as she added, "I guess this is about as close to him as I'm going to get."

"Fiona's still being . . . ?" I didn't know how to finish the sentence without being rude, so I just let it hang there.

"I don't know what her deal is," Jenelle confessed, a sharp edge of frustration in her voice. "I mean, I really like Anderson. But it's hard to get to know him when Fiona keeps getting in the way."

"Why don't you just tell her to get lost?" I asked.

Jenelle huffed out a sigh. "It's not that simple," she said.

"It seems like it is."

"It would be for *you*," Jenelle shot back. "But Fiona and I have been friends a long time."

I thought about that, and I knew Jenelle had a point. It wasn't easy to let go of a good friend. Even one with a mean streak. I decided to change the subject. "I've got boy issues, too," I said.

"That cutie — what's his name?" Jenelle asked.

"Scott."

"Right. What's up?"

"Good question. I barely see him anymore, and whenever I do, I'm usually screwing up the Academic Challenge somehow."

Jenelle grimaced. "Yikes."

"Tell me about it."

"Why don't you ask him to study or something?" Jenelle suggested.

"Tried it," I told her. "Bombfest."

"'Scuse me, y'all," said a voice behind us. In a moment, Brooke burst onto the stage in a vibrant fuchsia outfit. She put one hand on her hip and sashayed across the stage as the crowd went wild.

"She's doing so great," Jenelle said softly, almost to herself. She watched a moment longer, then turned to me. "Listen, I'm sure Scott's still into you," she said.

"What makes you say that?"

"I don't know — the way he was at Fiona's party." Jenelle shrugged. "You don't just stop feeling that way because someone gets the wrong answer to a trivia question."

I thought about that. It sounded right to me. "Thanks," I said, giving her a smile.

"You're welcome." Jenelle smiled back.

We stood there in the semidarkness for a few moments. There was something about the dim lighting and the chaos of the audience beyond the stage that made it seem as if Jenelle and I were standing on a patch of ground in an alternate universe. Like we had the place to ourselves. *I'm glad she's my friend,* I thought suddenly.

And in the next moment, we were swarmed as models rushed past us to get to the stage. The music blasted even louder for a moment as Fiona came out from behind the podium. The crowd went crazy. Jenelle let out a whistle and I clapped until my palms were red as everyone took a bow. The line of models looked amazing — like a clipping from *Vogue* magazine or something. They took another bow as the applause intensified. People leaped to their feet and didn't show any signs of slowing down.

"We are going to raise *so* much money," Jenelle said happily.

My face was starting to ache from smiling so hard, but I couldn't stop. This had turned out better than I'd hoped — even though I'd nearly missed the whole thing!

"Hey, y'all!" I said as I slipped into the booth across from Mitchie and Ķiwi on Monday morning. They were at their usual morning spot at the café, and the sweet steam from Kiwi's chai was wafting toward me. Behind us was a table full of girls dressed in mismatched plaid. Three of them had crazy crimped hair, and one of them was carrying a bag with a buckle on it. Jenelle had told me that the fund-raiser had raised more than thirty thousand dollars in one night. It certainly seemed like the Bounce look had exploded all over campus — practically everyone on my bus had been wearing the new look.

I was just about to tell my friends the good news when the words died in my throat. Kiwi was flashing me a worried look. "What is it?" I asked as she glanced over at Mitchie.

"Can I talk to you for a minute?" Mitchie asked me.

You know when the way someone says something can send a chill right through you? That was what happened to me at that moment. It was something about her tone and those words — *can I talk to you* — they gave me a sinking feeling at the center of my gut. "Sure," I said carefully. "What's up?"

Mitchie jerked her head toward the café exit. "The Challenge team is having a meeting." She grabbed a glossy magazine from the table and tucked it under her arm as she slid out of the booth.

I followed, looking back over my shoulder at Kiwi. Her long auburn hair was twisted up into a messy knot and secured with chopsticks and wavy wisps of hair framed her face. Her brown eyes looked huge in her pale face as she gave me a little smile. I think it was meant to be encouraging, but it wavered slightly, which only made me more stressed. I felt stretched — like a rubber band that someone was about to shoot across the room. "What's this about?" I asked as Mitchie led me down the hall, toward the science wing.

"Karter," Mitchie replied, and I relaxed a little.

Okay, I told myself as Mitchie yanked on the silver handle to Mr. Pearl's room. *No big deal. We probably just need to talk about study schedules and strategy and stuff.* Mr. Pearl was seated behind his desk, and Preston and Scott were standing beside him . . . but neither one of them looked up when we entered. Preston stared at a point on the floor, and Scott shifted from one foot to the other nervously as we walked toward the front of the room.

It was the first time that I'd been this close to Scott and hadn't felt the familiar butterfly flutter in my chest at the sight of him. In fact, the look on his face was sending a definite sinking feeling through my gut. *Something tells me that we're not going to discuss study schedules.*

"Ms. Flowers, good morning," Mr. Pearl said, toying with the handle of his coffee mug. "Wonderful that you could join us. Thank you." Mr. Pearl usually talks as if everything he says needs an exclamation point . . . but not right then. It was periods all the way.

"Hi." I put my bag down on a desk and waited. "So . . ."

Scott looked at Preston, who continued to stare at the floor. Then he turned to Mr. Pearl, who gave him an encouraging nod. Apparently, though, Scott didn't want to be the one to speak, because he turned to Mitchie and cleared his throat. She just glared back at him.

"Um, does anyone want to tell me what this is about?" I asked.

Mitchie sighed. "Look, Amy. It's just — it's just that it's become really clear that the Challenge isn't your . . . thing."

"Not that it couldn't be!" Mr. Pearl interjected. "You're a wonderful student! Wonderful!"

"But if we want to win, we all have to have our heads in the game," Mitchie went on. "And your head has been somewhere else."

"My head is in the game," I protested. Weakly. Mitchie had a point, and I knew it.

Mitchie pulled the magazine from under her arm, and I saw it for what it was — the most recent issue of the *Allington Observer*. She flipped to the center layout, which was all photos of the Fashion Fund-raiser.

I couldn't help noticing that there seemed to be more photos of Brooke than anybody else. There was a huge one of her in pink check-and-striped tights under the title "Funky Fashion Raises Funds!" I smiled a little.

Mitchie pointed to the photo. "This is where your head has been," she said. "Look, we think it would be best if Arielle took your place on the team."

I felt all of the air drain out of my body — my head felt light. "What?" I whispered. "You all feel . . ."

"The three of us voted," Mitchie explained. "It was two to one."

"You voted against me?" I whispered. I mean, it was hardly a surprise that Preston would vote against me. He couldn't stand me. But Mitchie? I could hardly believe it.

But Mitchie didn't deny it. She didn't say, "No,

153

no — I would never do that!" She just looked at me with her head cocked, as if she didn't know what to say.

I looked at Preston, but he didn't look up. Scott was playing with a paper clip on Mr. Pearl's desk. "But the Fashion Fund-raiser is over —"

"And so is our study time," Mitchie shot back. Her words were clipped, and even though she wasn't using a harsh voice or yelling or anything, they felt like a slap. "We face off against Karter tomorrow. We're going to need our strongest team . . . and that means Arielle."

Mr. Pearl took a swig of coffee and cleared his throat. "Ms. Flowers, this isn't meant as an insult. It's just that it has become clear to everyone that you were stretched too thin, that's all. Now is simply not your moment."

"No . . ." I murmured. I'd missed out on the fund-raiser, and now I was going to miss out on the Challenge finals. And Mitchie had stabbed me in the back. I felt mad and sad and hurt all at once. And then I pictured Arielle with a smug little smile on her face using her dumb Speed Spout Method, and I felt ready to strangle her. "I guess it really isn't my moment," I said at last.

Not at all.

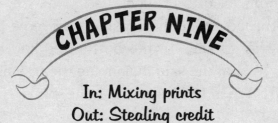

CHAPTER NINE

In: Mixing prints
Out: Stealing credit

I placed the blue glass bottle of sparkling water on
my tray and — without thinking — headed straight
for the Sunflower Room. I was two steps from the
door when I stopped in my tracks. I could see
the back of Mitchie's head from where I stood —
she was chatting with Kiwi, who hadn't noticed
me yet. Quickly, I ducked to the side of the doorway, hesitating. *How can I eat lunch with Mitchie
after she kicked me off the Challenge team? Are we
even speaking to each other right now?*

I didn't know the answers to the questions —
and I wasn't sure I wanted to know.

I stood there, weighing my options for a moment, and then I spotted Scott heading into the Fern Room. "Scott!" I called.

He turned suddenly, causing the crème brûlée on his tray to slide to the bottom lip and nearly fall off. "Whoa," he said, balancing the tray against his body. When he looked up at me, his eyes were round.

"Hey." Normally, I might have felt shy about inviting myself to sit with Scott. After all, he still had dreamy eyes and a sweet, shy smile. But he was also my only ally on the Challenge team. I wanted to show him that I knew it wasn't his fault that Mitchie and Preston had voted me off.

"Um . . . hi." He tried to smile, but it came out looking like more of a wince. "I'm kind of surprised you're talking to me," he said after a moment.

"You mean the Challenge thing?" I asked. "No big deal, really."

Scott nodded slowly, like he wasn't really following what I was saying. "Right."

"Where are you sitting?" I asked. "Mind if I join you?"

"Uh . . ." Scott stared down at his tray. "Actually, I was just going to inhale this and then dash to the library."

"Oh." I tried to keep the disappointment out of my voice.

"Sorry. . . . Hey, I'll catch up with you later, okay?" he said. Then he turned and hurried off.

"See you," I said faintly, but he'd already disappeared into the Fern Room. *Great*, I thought. Now I only had two options: sit by myself (no, thanks) or sit with my other good friend, Jenelle. Which meant sitting with the League.

Oh, well, I thought as I dragged my feet toward the Dahlia Room. *Lucia, at least, has been really nice to me lately. And we could talk about the fund-raiser.*

The League usually sat by themselves at a long table by the windows. But today, the table was packed. A few girls were even eating their food standing up at the end of the table near Fiona. Most of them were wearing clothes from the fund-raiser, and half of them had the new claw buckle-clasp bags. A little seed of envy burned in my stomach. It was ironic that I had organized the whole event, but I couldn't even afford any of the clothes.

"It's just that fashion has gotten so tame, you know?" Fiona was saying as I approached the table. "I really thought it was time to mix things up. That's why I went crazy mixing

157

the patterns — it was time to do something *different*."

"That was *so* brilliant," said a girl wearing a teal polka-dot skirt and striped tights.

"Solid colors are over," agreed another.

Jenelle shot me a smile as I squeezed my tray onto the last few inches of bare space at the far end of the table.

"That's why we decided to get models from all over the school, you know?" Fiona went on. "I mean, we all know that Alicia Reynolds and Noelle Abramson are professional models. So what? I, personally, wanted to see some new faces up there."

What? I gaped at Fiona in disbelief. *Is she serious? She was the one who tried to keep all of the "different-looking" models off the catwalk!*

"Brilliant," Polka-Dot-Skirt Girl said. "*So* brilliant. That was what made the show!" The rest of the table murmured agreement.

Jenelle and I exchanged a glance. I think she could see that I was too shocked to speak, because she piped up, "Actually, Fiona, I think that was Amy's suggestion."

Thank you.

But Fiona just laughed, like, "Right." Then she looked at me and said, "Mmm." It wasn't even a word — just a syllable — but somehow she managed to say, "Does anyone actually believe that Amy Flowers could have an idea like that?" without actually saying it.

The table full of girls tittered a bit, a few of them casting "Who are you, again?" looks in my direction. I felt my face burning. After all, nobody had seen me on the stage at the fund-raiser. All they saw was Fiona calling the show and taking a big fat bow.

"I think it's really amazing that you donated some of the money to the Book Fund," said Polka-Dot-Skirt Girl, who was clearly dying to be Fiona's new best friend.

Fiona gave her a heavy-lidded look. "It's *really important* to help people less fortunate than ourselves," she said. She touched her fingertip delicately to the edge of her glossy, pouty mouth.

"Charity is the new must-have accessory?" Lucia chimed in. "It's, like, more important than a Marc Jacobs bag?"

I rolled my eyes as the table let out a series of "mm-hmms" and "so trues."

Fiona flashed a triumphant little smile in my direction.

I can't believe I ever spent a single second feeling sorry for you! I thought. I worked my rear end off for that fund-raiser and I got kicked off the Challenge team . . . and for what? So Fiona could take all of the credit? I picked slightly at the herb-encrusted tilapia on my plate. It looked delicious, but I'd lost my appetite.

All of that work . . . for nothing.

"Fiona, do you think long hair will be in for spring?" asked a girl with a chin-length bob. "I'm thinking of growing it out."

"Short," Fiona said, taking a delicate bite of her steak salad.

"Ohs" rippled around the table, and I pictured half of the school hacking off their hair by the end of the week.

"Excuse me," I mumbled, grabbing my empty glass bottle. I couldn't stand to sit there for another minute.

I headed into the serving area, where I dropped the bottle into a recycling bin and reached for a mug. *I think I'll try some chai*, I thought, heading for the coffee and tea bar. Kiwi always said that it had calming effects.

I placed my order and was just sipping the warm cinnamony-milky blend when Brooke Rosen appeared behind me. "Amy!" she said when I turned around. She was grinning hugely, revealing the dimples in her cheeks.

"Hey, Brooke." Honestly, I felt like her grin was spreading straight from her face to mine. Between her huge smile and the delicious tea, I was definitely feeling better.

"I thought I saw you dash in here!" she said warmly. "I just wanted to thank you for letting me be in the fund-raiser. What a blast! I know that Fiona never would have let me in if it weren't for you."

I shrugged. "She says she would have."

Brooke snorted. "She didn't last year."

I didn't know what to say to that, so I just said, "You were the hit of the show." I really meant it.

"The show was the hit," Brooke corrected. "I was only a little part of it. And as a thank-you . . ." She held up an oversized pale yellow shopping bag stuffed with tissue paper.

A warm feeling spread from my head to my toes. "You didn't have to do that," I said as I placed my tea mug on the dark teak bar and reached inside.

"I wanted to," Brooke said. "I know you're a bag person, so . . ."

"Oh . . ." My voice was breathless as I pulled out a bright orange bag with a buckle clasp and tons of pockets. It was huge — exactly the size I would have picked for myself, so I can haul around all of my stuff. "It's *gorgeous*."

"You really like it? Because I saved the receipt, and you can exchange —"

"I love it," I said, cutting her off. Then I did something that I think neither one of us expected — I wrapped Brooke Rosen in a huge bear hug. "Thank you," I whispered into her mass of curly hair.

She was so surprised that she laughed a little, but she hugged me back. "You're welcome," she said.

I pulled back to smile at her, but her face blurred — I was actually starting to tear up. I don't know — I guess I was just so grateful that *someone* thought I'd done a good job.

Brooke looked down at my mug of tea. "What is that?" she asked. "It smells awesome."

"It's chai," I told her. "My friend Kiwi drinks it all the time."

"Hm," Brooke said. "I guess I'd better try it." She grinned at me. "It always pays to try new things."

I thought about that. I'd been trying a lot of new things lately, and none of them had really turned out the way I'd hoped. The Fashion Fundraiser had gone well, but Fiona had stolen the credit. And the Challenge had turned into a complete disaster. But Brooke's smile was so contagious and I was so thrilled with the sweet present she had given me that I couldn't be totally negative. "Maybe you're right," I said.

Brooke gave me a playful punch in the arm. "I always am," she joked. Then she winked and walked off.

"There you are!" said a voice behind me. "Omigosh! What are you drinking?"

Turning, I saw Kiwi's sparkling brown eyes smiling at me. "Is that . . . *chai tea*?"

"It's really good," I told her, taking a sip.

"It's the best," Kiwi agreed warmly. "So, where are you sitting? Why aren't you with us?"

I wasn't sure how to answer, so I looked down into my milky drink and inhaled a long, cinnamon-y-breath. "Maybe you should ask Mitchie," I said.

Kiwi laid a gentle hand on my arm. "She told me about the team."

"I feel like she stabbed me in the back." I was surprised at the tightness in my chest as I said the words. I hadn't realized just how upset I was.

Kiwi nodded. "I'll bet. I'd feel the same. Mitchie feels really awful about it."

"She does?" For some reason, that surprised me. "Then why did she do it?"

Kiwi set her greenish-blue mug on the counter and placed a teabag in it, then poured in some hot water. "This Academic Challenge thing is really important to her — and she's seriously stressing about it," Kiwi said as she added some honey to her mint tea. "You know, everyone in Mitchie's family is always comparing her to Akina. If Mitchie brings home a B, they want to know why she couldn't get an A — like her sister. Her parents think of Akina as the smart one . . ."

". . . and Mitchie wants to prove them wrong," I said slowly.

Her right shoulder rose and dipped in a mini-shrug. "Wouldn't you?"

"I guess . . . but I don't know if I'd kick my friend off the Challenge team to do it."

"Mitchie didn't think you'd care so much." The corner of Kiwi's mouth tucked up into an ironic smile. "You really shocked her this morning when you got upset. She told me that she'd actually thought she was doing you a favor — giving you a break. She thought you'd be relieved."

I took a long, slow sip of my tea, letting the warmth from the liquid spread through my body. What Kiwi was saying made a lot of sense. And, in a way, I really *was* relieved that I didn't have to study for the Challenge anymore. It was making science — my favorite subject — seem seriously un-fun. "Maybe she was right," I said.

"You should talk to her," Kiwi suggested.

"Yeah . . ." I tapped the edge of my heavy ceramic mug with a fingernail, hesitating. I felt like I'd already apologized to Mitchie a thousand times in the past week. Sorry I'm late. Sorry I didn't know the answer. Sorry I blew the Challenge. I was sick of talking. *Still*, I thought. *Kiwi is right. Mitchie needs her friends right now.*

I wanted to do something special to show her that I wasn't mad about the Challenge — and that I really wanted her to win. But what could I do?

Suddenly, I had an idea. It was the perfect way to *show* Mitchie my support — literally.

CHAPTER TEN

In: Banners
In: Brains
In: BFFs

Kirk looked around the auditorium, which was rapidly filling with people. "Tell me again why I'm doing this," he said, eyeing the TV crew near the stage.

"Because you're the most wonderful brother ever," I told him as I unfolded the bedsheet I'd painted the night before. GO, ALLINGTON! it read. BEAT THEIR BRAINS!

"That doesn't sound like me," Kirk pointed out.

"You're also doing it because I promised not to tell Dad how the Dondelo got broken."

"Oh, right." Kirk nodded. The last time it rained, he'd used our dad's prized sculpture to dry out a pair of muddy socks.

"Why did you turn it on, anyway?" I asked him.

"I thought the socks would dry faster," he said. I handed him the sheet and he rolled his eyes. "This isn't a sporting event, you know. We're the only people here who have a banner."

I gave him a dubious look. "This from the guy who painted his face blue to go watch his school's production of *Grease*?"

"Dan was in the show!" Kirk insisted. "I wanted to show support!"

"Well, Mitchie's on the Challenge team," I said, handing him half of the sheet. "Hold it high."

Kirk looked down at the banner, then up at the stage. Mitchie was standing on the left side with Preston and Scott. For a minute, Kirk looked like he might refuse. "Well . . ." he said at last, "since it's Mitchie . . ."

Just then, Mitchie turned her head and looked in our direction. Mild surprise registered on her features, and I held the banner in front of me. "Hold it up!" I whispered to Kirk. "Higher!"

Obediently, he raised his end of the banner so that it was taut between us. Mitchie squinted for a

167

moment, and then a wide smile broke out over her face. She gestured for me to come over, and a cool, happy feeling shot through me.

"I'm going to go say hi," I told my brother, shoving my half of the banner at him. "I'll be right back." I scurried toward the stage and up the steps.

"You came," Mitchie said warmly, wrapping me in a hug.

"I wouldn't have missed it," I told her. "I want to see you guys put a hurt on Karter." I batted my eyes innocently and gave her a goofy smile.

Mitchie bit her lip for a moment. "Listen, I'm really sorry about . . . everything. By the time I realized it was stupid and I shouldn't have done it, it was too late."

I shook my head. "I screwed up, too. So we're even." We stood there for an awkward moment. Usually, I can find a ton of things to say to Mitchie . . . but at that moment, I had to wrack my brain to come up with, "So, how are you feeling?"

Mitchie sucked in her breath. "Okay, I guess. I just hope we win, after all of this drama."

"You'd better win," I told her. "I made you a banner!"

She laughed. "Yeah, and dragged your brother along to hold it up."

"He wanted to come," I lied.

Mitchie folded her arms across her chest. "Really," she said dryly.

I was about to tell her that it was better than his alternatives when I felt a gentle hand on my arm. When I realized that the fingers belonged to Scott, I felt a shot of electricity run through me. But he didn't look happy to see me. Instead, he looked worried. Preston was standing beside him, holding a cell phone in his left hand.

"What is it?" Mitchie asked, reading Scott's face.

"It's Arielle," he said, looking over her shoulder. "She can't make it."

"What?" Mitchie cried. "Why not?"

"She's got laryngitis," Preston explained. He played absently with his green-and-blue-striped tie. "That stupid Speed Spout Method ruined her voice."

"If we don't have a full team, we're disqualified," Scott pointed out.

"Okay." Mitchie ran her hand through her hair. "Okay. Okay. This isn't a problem." She turned to me. "You'll do it, right?"

For a minute, I wasn't sure what she was asking. Then I got it. "Of course."

Mitchie's eyes were shining. "Cool."

"I knew you'd come through for us," Preston said, which surprised me so much that I didn't say anything back. Which was just as well, because a bald man in a navy sport coat was gesturing for us to take our places. He was carrying a clipboard. He signaled to the cameraman and then held up his hand, signaling that we had five seconds, then four, then three . . .

I looked out at the audience at Kirk, who was giving me a "What's going on?" look. I shrugged and pointed at Mitchie. Kirk folded his arms across his chest and kept the GO, ALLINGTON! sign bunched up on his lap.

A familiar-looking older guy began speaking into the TV camera in a smooth voice. "Hello, Challenge fans — and welcome to the Lone Star State! I'm Lawrence Fuller, and I'm hosting this Houston edition, where Karter will take on Allington Academy. It's sure to be a showdown!" He grinned hugely, then turned to face us. "All right, everyone, let's get started!"

I took a deep breath. *It's going to be okay,* I told myself, trying not to think about the fact that I hadn't done a nanosecond of studying for the past twenty-four hours. I looked over at the Karter team. The leader was a tall blond girl with a spray of freckles across her cheeks. She was standing beside a dark-skinned boy with a large nose and huge eyes. There were two other boys — one with a mop of curly black hair, and one with hair so pale that his eyebrows were invisible. They looked confident. *Very* confident.

And, suddenly, I wasn't feeling so confident myself.

We were standing behind a counter so that nobody saw when Mitchie snaked her pinkie finger around mine and gave a little squeeze. I squeezed back, which made me feel a little better. *After all,* I thought, *it's not like I'm up here alone. Mitchie and Scott are with me. And Preston. For what he's worth.*

"All right," Mr. Fuller said, turning to Karter. "First question goes to our top-scoring team. How does one calculate the area of an equilateral triangle?"

And — like that — we were off.

Karter was really good. They didn't miss a single question in the first section. On the other hand, neither did we. Even *I* was rocking my game. *Maybe studying is overrated*, I thought as I answered my fourth question in a row. "Anthropod," I said.

"Correct!" Mr. Fuller beamed and the audience clapped.

"Awesome," Mitchie whispered, just loud enough for me to hear as Mr. Fuller asked Karter a question about Emily Dickinson.

"Well, viewers, this is only the third time in Challenge history that we've had two teams that haven't missed a single question in our opening round," Mr. Fuller announced. "Let's give them a big hand, shall we?" The audience erupted. That was when I noticed that there was a whole Allington section at the back — it looked like Brooke Rosen and Voe Silk and a bunch of other girls from the fund-raiser were cheering for us. Even Kirk was getting into the action — he was holding up the banner. Of course, with only one person, all you could read was GO, ALL. Which, I thought, showed good sportsmanship.

Once the applause had died down, Mr. Fuller explained the rules of the final round. "This round consists of only three questions, and both teams must answer the same questions. Each team will be allowed to confer for a moment before they write their answer on the screen provided. All right? Let's go. First question: What was the capital of Egypt during the time that the Great Pyramid was being built?"

We all leaned in toward each other. "Cairo?" Scott asked, but Preston shook his head.

"Memphis," he said.

"Memphis?" Mitchie repeated. "Like Memphis, Tennessee?"

Preston looked amused. "Where do you think they got the name?"

Mitchie looked doubtful, but she wrote down the word using the touch screen in front of us.

Karter revealed their answer first. "Memphis," said the crazy-haired boy, and the word appeared on the giant screen behind him.

"That is correct," Mr. Fuller said. *Excellent. They had it right, but so did we.* I looked over at Preston and smiled. He smiled back — a little shyly, I thought. Then he turned away, touching his tie tentatively.

We revealed our answer, then we moved on to the next question. "Who is the only president of the United States to be sworn into office by his father?"

It was Scott who knew the answer, so we let him announce it. "Calvin Coolidge," he said as the name appeared in Mitchie's handwriting on the screen behind his head.

"Correct," Mr. Fuller said.

Unfortunately, Karter got it right, too.

"All right, final question," Mr. Fuller said, glancing down at the white card in his hand. "In the 1660s, there was a new fashion in English footwear. What was it?"

I turned to Mitchie, our history expert, but she looked pale. She glanced at me, then Preston, then back at me. "I—I don't know," she said. "Maybe . . ." She shook her head.

I felt as if my heart had fallen out of my chest. *How can she not know?* I thought. *Mitchie knows everything about history!* Panic washed over me, quick, like an unexpected wave. I glanced out at the audience for a moment, and my eye fell on my brother. The chair beside him was empty, except for my brand-new purse — the one with the buckle clasp. Suddenly, something echoed in my mind. Something Jenelle had said . . .

In a flash, I grabbed the stylus from Mitchie's hand. "What — what are you —"

But I didn't have a chance to answer her, because at that moment, Mr. Fuller said, "Time. Karter, do you have an answer?"

The dark-skinned boy closed his eyes slowly. "High heels?" he said as the words flashed up behind him.

Mr. Fuller looked down at his card. "I'm sorry," he said. "That is not correct."

There was a gasp from the audience, and my heart thudded against my ribs.

"Allington, if you get this question right, you will have won the Academic Challenge. The question is, 'In the 1660s, there was a new fashion in English footwear. What was it?'"

"Buckles," I said as the word flashed up on the screen behind me.

"That is correct," Mr. Fuller said. "Allington Academy, you've just won this year's Academic Challenge!" And the next thing I knew, Mitchie had grabbed me, and Preston was giving me a high five. Scott was grinning, and my brother was jumping up and down in the audience, waving the banner like a flag. Mr. Fuller gave us a trophy that was the size of my four-year-old cousin, Arthur, and then Mr. Pearl came over to thump us all on the back and exclaim, "Wonderful! Wonderful!" over and over.

"Congratulations," said a smooth voice near my ear, and I saw Mitchie's face beam proudly as Mr. Pearl pulled Akina into our group.

"Akina Ohara!" he cried happily. "How is my star pupil? It's wonderful to see you here! Delightful!"

Akina laced a lock of hair delicately around her

small ear as she said, "I'm so happy that Allington finally won again."

"Thanks to your sister!" Mr. Pearl patted Mitchie's shoulder. Mitchie smiled at Akina.

"Not on that last question," Akina pointed out. "I thought you were on the team for literature and *history*, Michiko."

The smile disappeared from Mitchie's face.

"Mitchie got more questions right than anyone else on the team," I said quickly. "If it weren't for her, we wouldn't have made it to the finals in the first place."

"True, true!" Mr. Pearl agreed. "The Ohara sisters are stars!"

Akina arched an eyebrow at me, but she didn't say anything. Mitchie looked like she wanted to hug me, though. *Good.*

This was her moment. She'd earned it. *And*, I realized as I looked around at the rest of my team — Scott and Preston and even Mr. Pearl — *so had the rest of us.*

And nobody could take that away.

"I don't know how you can eat that," Mitchie said, scrunching up her face and frowning at my bowl.

"Mmmm!" I said, digging my spoon deeper into the gooey peanut butter sauce that was quickly

176

turning my chocolate ice cream into soup. I slipped the spoon into my mouth and pried my lips apart long enough to say. "Delicious!"

"Peanut butter belongs on sandwiches — not ice cream," Mitchie harumphed, but she grinned at me.

"I know you're just trying to get me to give you a bite," I said. I pushed my bowl slightly toward her. "Try it."

Mitchie lifted her eyebrows and opened her mouth, as if she was about to protest, then seemed to think again. "Okay," she said, shoving her bowl toward me. "You can try mine, too."

I dug my spoon into her bowl of dulce de leche ice cream with hot fudge. "Wow, that's good," I said when I tasted it. "What do you think of the peanut butter?"

"Way better than I expected," Mitchie admitted. "But I think I like mine better."

"Me too." I licked the sticky sauce off of my spoon happily and gazed around at the Purple Cow, my favorite ice-cream place. It had a black-and-white cow motif and purple booths, and served the best ice cream in Houston. The place smelled amazing, too. The owner, Jackie, was always cooking up waffle cones. Just to tempt me, I think.

"So . . . have you recovered from everything yet?" Mitchie asked. "The Fashion Fund-raiser and the Challenge?"

"We just won the Challenge last night," I said. "Give me a few hours."

Mitchie laughed. "All right, Superwoman," she joked. "I guess you can have a little break. After all, you did save the day. Big-time. I mean, Preston said you would all along."

I cocked my head, not sure I'd heard her right. "He — what?"

"Preston kept telling me and Scott that you were going to come through," Mitchie explained. "He said you were just busy with the fund-raiser, and you'd get it together." She playfully snuck another spoonful of my ice cream, but I barely noticed — I was too busy trying to comprehend her words.

Preston Harringford . . .

Preston had said that I was going to come through?

That was weird. Beyond weird. But even weirder was what it meant. Because Mitchie had told me that the team voted — two to one — to replace me with Arielle.

Two to one. And Preston had wanted me to stay.

But that meant . . .

. . . that meant *Scott* had voted with Mitchie to kick me off the team. My head felt like it was full of fuzz. All of this time, I'd been thinking of Scott as my Almost-Boyfriend. We'd danced together at Fiona's party. He'd asked me out on a Kind-of Date. I pictured his smile — how one tooth at the top slightly overlapped the other. . . .

"You okay?" Mitchie asked, looking at me carefully.

"Yeah," I said dimly. "Fine."

"Because you look like someone just hypnotized you," Mitchie went on.

"No, I —" But I couldn't finish the sentence. I just shook my head. "I'm fine," I said, forcing myself to take another spoonful of ice cream. "I just — I just thought of something, that's all." What I was thinking was, *Scott never apologized for voting against me. Mitchie and I made up. But Scott never said anything. . . .*

Just then, the bell over the door jingled, and a girl in a red jacket, black top, and long black scarf flounced in. She tossed her long black hair and strode toward the ice-cream counter. It was Fiona. Lucia was right behind her, being trailed by a guy with a huge video camera marked ACTION NEWS. "I'd like to speak to the manager," Fiona said.

"Are you here to pick up the ice cream?" Jackie asked, casting a self-conscious glance at the camera. She wiped her hands quickly on a purple towel and straightened her black-and-white-cow-splotch apron.

"Absolutely," Fiona said in a sickly sweet voice. "Thank you *so* much for your generous donation. The soup kitchen is *so* grateful."

"They don't, like, usually get ice cream for dessert?" Lucia chimed in. "This is going to be the best meal ever?"

"We've managed to get several local restaurants to agree to donate food once a month," Fiona explained. "Including Azteca."

Lucia gave a tight little smile as the cameraman turned to her. Azteca was one of the restaurants that her family owned. "'Home of the Bodacious Burrito'?" Lucia added, flashing a smile at the lens.

I looked over at Mitchie, who was staring at Fiona as if she had just announced that she was visiting from another planet. Her face was so funny that I gave a little giggle-snort.

The door jingled again and Jenelle held it open for three guys rolling dollies. "This way," she said, gesturing them inside. When she saw me, she waved.

"What's going on?" Mitchie asked as I waved back.

"No clue," I admitted just as Fiona strode up to our table.

"Hello, Amy," she said. She didn't say hello to Mitchie.

"Um. Hi."

"Oh, what's this?" Fiona batted her long lashes in mock surprise as she pulled a glossy magazine from the black bag slung over her shoulder. "Why, it's the latest copy of the *Allington Observer*!" She flipped past the Fashion Fund-raiser photos to a page marked with an orange Post-it. "Read it and weep," she said, handing it over to me.

I read the headline aloud: "Allington Students Get Fabulous — With Charity."

Mitchie leaned in to scan the article. "You're helping a soup kitchen?" she asked doubtfully.

"Mmm." Fiona pressed her lips together primly. "Don't you know? Charity is the new accessory." She snapped her fingers in my general direction. "And I guess you're not the only one with style," she said, then stalked to the door. Lucia held it open and Fiona flounced out, followed by the three guys with dollies. Each was stacked with four large tubs of ice cream.

"Charity is the new accessory?" Mitchie repeated. She stared at me, wide-eyed. "Is she serious?"

"I think so," I said, trying to hide my smile.

Mitchie turned to look out the window and into the parking lot, where the guys were piling the ice cream into the trunk of a limo. Fiona was directing. "Does it matter that she's doing good deeds for all the wrong reasons?" Mitchie asked.

I thought about that for a moment. Okay, so Fiona had stolen my idea about charity. But that didn't bother me. At least this way, everyone was a winner. Fiona was happy, the soup kitchen was happy. . . . If she was going to be obnoxious, at least it was for a good cause. "I guess not."

"Hey, guys," Jenelle said softly. She had approached our table so quietly that I hadn't even noticed she was standing there until she spoke. "Congratulations on the Challenge." She dug her hands into the pockets of the plaid jacket she was wearing. "I watched you on TV."

"Oh, *Celebrity Makeover* was canceled?" Mitchie said snidely.

Jenelle's face fell.

"Thanks, Jenelle," I said quickly, giving Mitchie a warning look. *What was that comment for?* I thought. *Jenelle was just trying to be nice!*

Mitchie stared back at me for a moment, then seemed to thaw slightly. "Yeah," she said finally. "Yeah, thanks."

"I couldn't believe you guys knew the answers to all of those questions," Jenelle went on. "Half of them were about stuff I'd never even heard of."

"Well, we wouldn't have won if it wasn't for you," I said. Jenelle looked confused. "You're the one who told me about buckles on shoes," I reminded her. "How they came into fashion in the seventeenth century."

"Really?" Mitchie asked.

Jenelle blushed, and she looked like she was about to say something when a horn blared from the parking lot. Fiona was standing beside the limo, leaning on the horn while the driver stared at her in shock. Fiona's words were muffled through the glass, but it looked like she was shouting, "Come on!"

"I'd better go," Jenelle said quickly. "Congratulations again!" And a moment later, she'd scurried out to the limo and climbed inside.

"Wow," Mitchie said after a moment. "I never would have guessed that Jenelle had anything useful in her brain."

"You don't know her," I said. "Not as well as you think you do." It was funny — Mitchie had said those exact words to me just a few weeks ago. But I felt like she was wrong. I *did* know Jenelle. Mitchie was the one who wouldn't give Jenelle a chance.

Mitchie watched as the limo pulled out of the parking lot, its red taillights blending into the rest of the heavy Houston traffic. "Maybe you're right," she said at last. "Maybe I don't."

I didn't want to make a big deal about it, so I didn't say anything as I took another bite of my ice cream. Still, I was smiling behind my spoon. *Who knows?* I thought. *Maybe one day Mitchie will be able to forgive Jenelle. . . .*

Which sure would make my life easier.

Hey, a girl can dream, right?

CANDY APPLE BOOKS
Fresh. Fun. Sweet. Take a Bite!

The Accidental Cheerleader by Mimi McCoy

The Boy Next Door by Laura Dower

Miss Popularity by Francesco Sedita

How to Be a Girly Girl in Just Ten Days by Lisa Papademetriou

Drama Queen by Lara Bergen

The Babysitting Wars by Mimi McCoy

Totally Crushed by Eliza Willard

I've Got a Secret by Lara Bergen

Callie for President by Robin Wasserman

Making Waves by Randi Reisfeld and H.B. Gilmour

The Sister Switch by Jane B. Mason and Sarah Hines Stephens

Accidentally Fabulous by Lisa Papademetriou

Confessions of a Bitter Secret Santa by Lara Bergen

Read them all!

■ SCHOLASTIC

www.scholastic.com/candyapple

CANDYBL13

Is her fate written in the stars?

Abby's life was perfect—until a trip to an astrologer gets her hooked on reading her horoscope, and suddenly, things go awry. Do the stars have it in for her?